AF348403

CLOUD COVER

CLOUD COVER

A Novel

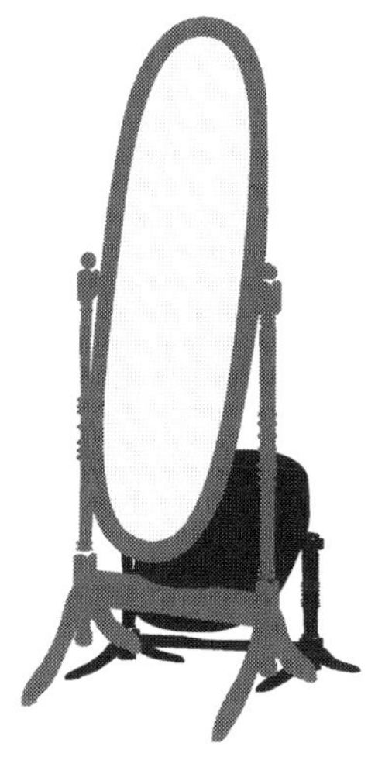

Jeffrey Sotto

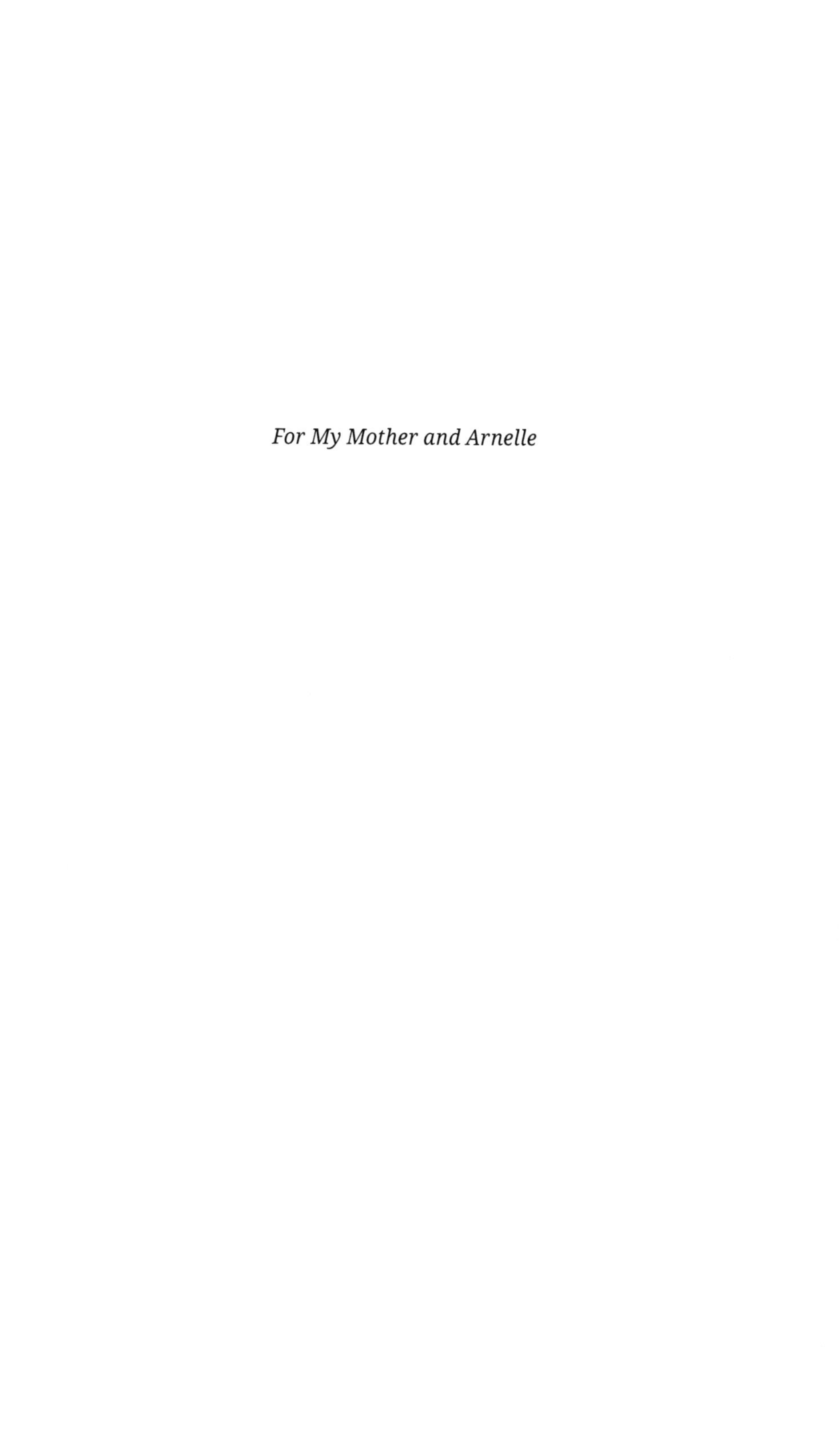

For My Mother and Arnelle

Dear Reader,

Thank you for your interest in this story. Some of the more unsettling and potentially triggering contents of the book are intended to show, with full transparency, the perspective of someone suffering from a disordered state of mental and physical health. It is not my intention to endorse the behaviours of the character(s), but to portray them realistically.

I thank you once again.

Prologue

Chapter 1: Yellow

April 2010

My boyfriend, Ken, said he found me attractive because he thought I looked like Bruno Mars. I didn't see it at first. As his songs got more popular, people started to make comments to me about it. Ken joked that if I wore a fedora, sunglasses and chains, and walked everywhere surrounded by big guys that looked like bodyguards, I could pass as him on the street. On top of that, I had that "extra bit of pudge, just like Bruno," he'd say.

Except for that last one, I liked the comments. It was nice to see someone famous who wasn't conventionally handsome with a square jaw and pointy nose. Bruno is half Filipino, a quarter Puerto Rican, and a quarter Jewish. Although I'm full Filipino, I felt we shared a sense of "otherness"; in a glamorous world of white, blue-eyed, blond-haired Justins (Timberlakes, Biebers...) and Kens (my boyfriend, *my* very own Ken doll), he stuck out with his round eyes, full cheeks and brown skin, a lot like my own features.

I too stood out in my gay Toronto world. And by stood out, I mean I was invisible. First of all, it was difficult to spot me in a crowd: I'm five feet and three-quarters-of-an-inch tall. In the dimly lit bars of Church Street, someone that short—usually of Asian descent and often referred to as "yellow"—would get lost in a sea of chests and armpits. Tall, beautifully sculpted, Caucasian "non-yellow" men would elbow my face by accident, and not even know it.

But Bruno Mars gave me the possibility that a yellow Asian could be cute, perhaps attractive. Maybe even, dare I say it... sexy?

Everyone always thought of me as "Tony, that nice guy," which was fine. To be admired was nice.

But to be desired meant more to me than I liked to admit.

"Tony?" a voice said. Fifteen-year-old Abigail caught me day dreaming at my desk. I looked up to a sea of eyes, all centred on me.

"Yes, Abigail?"

"Should I read out what I have now?"

"Of course."

The assignment was for the kids to write three-to-five sentences answering the question "Who am I?" There were no criteria, guidelines or restrictions. And no judgment. This was a creative writing class, after all.

"My name is Abigail. I am fifteen years old and in grade 10. I like writing. It makes me feel like an artist. My favourite movie is Legally Blonde. I think I want to be a lawyer, just like Elle Woods. Totally my hero."

She looked up at me, seeking approval.

"Great!" I said. "Thanks, Abigail, good work."

"That movie sucks!" a boy at the back of the class said. A few of the other kids laughed. Abigail rolled her eyes.

"Hey guys. No judgments in this class, okay?" I said. "We should feel free to share whatever we want without fear of being judged."

The class grew silent.

I continued. "And just for the record, Legally Blonde is an absolute masterpiece of cinema!" They all laughed. "Put yourself in Elle Woods' shoes! Empathize! How great would it feel to stick it to your stupid ex-boyfriend by getting in law school and upstaging him?

That's amazing, right?"

Many of the students giggled and nodded.

"Empathy, guys. I want you to consider all points of view when you write. It'll make you a better writer, and a better person."

Abigail smiled. "Tony?"

"Yes?"

"What about you? Don't you have to tell us who you are?"

I didn't have anything prepared. I scrambled some sentences together in my head:

I'm Tony, I'm 29. I wanted to be a writer when I was a kid. Now, I teach creative writing to teens at this community centre. So, I guess things didn't turn out exactly as planned. But I have my health. I have a boyfriend named Ken—a lawyer—who, when he isn't pinching my chubby cheeks calling me his "chunky monkey," is a good guy. Although we don't yet own multiple properties together, we go on vacations and occasionally eat at restaurants in Yorkville where the portions look like pebbles on their giant plates. But the photos look good on my Facebook. I guess that means my life is close to perfect, no?

But I kept my biography to myself. I looked back at Abigail and deflected the question: "This class is all about you guys, not me. I'm just here to help if I can."

There was a spring in my step when I left class to head home, which was a quaint little house in Little Portugal. Ken and I were celebrating our two-year anniversary. I'd been thinking about what to wear for this night for months. I wanted to look good for him. He deserved it; he worked his butt off and had recently made partner at his firm. I loved him.

I tried to channel Bruno's current 50s-doo-wop trend: I wore a dark blue suit with black lapel, shiny black shoes, a white shirt and a black tie. To finish the look, I teased my hair to get it as big and fluffy as possible, with a small curl dangling loosely on my forehead, as if I was carefree and cool.

In the last couple of months, I had been trying to lose some weight by cutting down on carbohydrates. I replaced my rice at meals with salad. Ken would comment every now and then about me "getting more doughy, but it's okay because it's cute." I was 130 pounds, with a normal (but on the high side of normal) BMI of 24.9. But I took his comments as a cue to trim myself, and I thought the new diet was working. I stood in front of the mirror, as I waited for him. *Okay, not bad.*

Ken was one of the most punctual people I knew, so it was odd to get an "I'm running late" text. He was never late.

We were going to the Toronto Symphony to see Rachmaninoff's Piano Concerto no. 2, my favourite, next to Vivaldi's Four Seasons. Ken preferred the less melodic, harsher classical music, like Shostakovich and the newer pieces by modern composers, which to me sounded like cats in a dryer. One of my best friends, Nick, said that we were too pretentious for late-twenty-something gay men, with our love of "old people music," as he put it. But I didn't like classical music because I liked being fancy; I liked it because it was simply beautiful. And all right, I'll be honest at the risk of sounding snooty—I thought anything was better than the simple beats and "grab-my-ass" lyrics of basic pop music.

Ken came in, looking as handsome as ever in a grey suit and gelled-back, dirty blonde hair, his blue eyes sparkling. *My Ken doll.* He was holding a bouquet of roses. They were yellow.

Yellow?

Why were they yellow?

"Hi babe," I said, "you look amazing."

"Thanks. Should we head out?"

"Let me just put the flowers in a vase."

Ken was uncharacteristically quiet in the car.

"So, how was your day?" I asked as he drove.

"Good," he answered.

"You okay? You're a little quiet."

"I'm fine. Can we just listen to the radio?"

"Sure."

He turned up the volume. Something was wrong. He hadn't even commented on my suit or how I looked at all.

I had made reservations at Sotto Sotto in Yorkville. According to *Toronto Life* magazine, it was one of "*the* places to eat." I tried to keep initiating conversation over dinner but couldn't get Ken to seem interested.

"It's going to be a great term," I said, trying to sound chipper. "The kids today were awesome. They loved the selection of poems I gave for homework. One of them told me that "Morning Song" by Sylvia Plath reminded her of her relationship with her mother, because both her mother and the mother in the poem weren't even sure they wanted children. She interpreted that on her own. Sometimes the kids just really just amaze me."

Ken was looking down at the floor. "I gotta go to the bathroom," he said, as he scurried from the table.

He came back ten minutes later, his eyes watering and cheeks red. His face was puffy.

"Ken, are you okay? You look like you just threw up," I said, concerned.

"I did," he replied.

"What, are you sick? Should we leave?"

"No, it's okay." He lowered his voice. "I need to talk to you."

"Okay. What's bothering you? You haven't been yourself all night."

"I need to tell you something."

"Yeah?"

"I've been thinking a lot lately. About us."

It was that line that you hear in movies and automatically know what's about to happen. But this wasn't the movies.

Suddenly I realized. The roses. They were yellow.

"Ken, why were the roses yellow?"

He shifted his eyes to the window. "They were bi-coloured. Did you not see they were yellow with specks of red on them?"

"What are you saying?"

His eyes met mine, and he said, "I realized something. I realized … that I love you, but only as a friend. That's why the roses were yellow, for friendship, but blended with red, for love."

I had no words. Maybe that was why I never made it as a writer.

I didn't want to believe it. This shouldn't be happening to me, I thought. I'm a good person. I'm nice and I care about people. I didn't deserve this.

But it all made sense. Over time, our conversations had become nothing but cold, dry one-liners. We were both getting busier at work. We hadn't had sex in months.

Then a question popped into my head. "Is there someone else?" I was afraid of the answer.

The response was worse than a "yes."

"No, there's nobody else. It's *you*. Don't get me wrong. You're an amazing guy, Tony. You work hard. The kids at the centre love you. I just don't feel that way about *you*. But someone will snatch you up in no time."

Was it sadder that he broke up with me, not for someone else, but because of me? That he only loved me as a friend (who also apparently made him vomit?). Is that like quitting your job, not because you found a better one but because you didn't care for it enough that *not* having a job was a better option?

We sat in silence for a few minutes.

"Are you okay?" he asked.

"No. You better go."

He got up and slowly exited the restaurant.

Other diners were stealing looks at me and then looking to their partners to probably discuss why I was suddenly alone at the table. The entrees had come just as Ken got up to leave. I picked up the fork and quickly shoveled my pasta into my face until the plate was clean. I even ate half of Ken's plate. It was too much for my stomach and I felt sick, but I kept stuffing the food in. Anything to numb what I was feeling. Anything to change the memory of this evening. I paid the bill and went to the symphony alone to try and fill my ears with anything other than his words. "It's *you*... I just don't feel that way about *you*."

Rachmaninoff's Piano Concerto no. 2 became the soundtrack for all the images in my head, all the dreams I had had of my life with Ken that now would never come to be: a condo on Lakeshore facing south; vacations to Gay Par-ee; grand dinner parties with friends where we would eat rack of lamb and discuss what films we hated at TIFF; running to tell him that I had finally got my writing published, and him picking me off the ground and spinning me in circles until I felt dizzy with hope and happiness and love. The montage of hazy dreams faded away into a single image of yellow roses, which would eventually wilt and die too.

Part One

Chapter 2: Ceremony

April 2015

Don't keep the food inside for too long. That was one of my many
rules.

"Tony, are you there? Hello?" Emily asked.

"What?" I said. I had to refocus. This girl was nice as can be, but I
had no idea what she was talking about.

"You zoned out there for a sec," she replied.

"Sorry, go on."

"Anyway. My title should be changed from office coordinator
to director, for God's sake! If it wasn't for me, that office would be a
disaster. I basically run the place!"

I couldn't listen to this girl anymore. I had to go. There was
something else on my mind.

"Excuse me, Emily. I'm feeling a little sick. Sorry." I turned
around quickly enough to avoid looking at her face or hearing her
response.

"Where's the washroom?" I asked some stranger, trying not to
sound frantic over the blaring music. I needed a toilet asap.

"Past the kitchen, end of the hall on the right," he said.

"Thanks."

I rushed to the end of the hallway to see a line of people waiting outside. Of course. A house party full of drunk millennials—there had to be a lineup for the bathroom.

Why did I come? Because Nick always was harping on me for not getting out enough. Because I figured it actually might be nice to socialize.

It was finally my turn. The cramped bathroom was a mess. Hair on the floor and in the sink. Clutter all over the counter. I looked down at the toilet. Seat up, piss on the rim, and little pieces of shit stuck to the inside of the bowl.

I can't do this here.

But then I thought about all that I had shoved in my face in the previous two hours: pigs in a blanket, pizza, brie and crackers, chips, cupcakes, sushi rolls, nachos and about six hands full of M&Ms. This was not a fancy, grown-up dinner party, but I didn't care. I came thinking I would socialize, but really all I wanted was to stuff myself. I was so full it was hard to breathe.

I can't do this here.

Then the fear consumed me. All that food—easily between 1,800 and 2,000 calories—would soon become fat and redistribute itself on my hips, ass, stomach and face. My cheeks would get full again just as they'd been six years ago, earning them pinches and the lovely nickname "chunky monkey." The food needed to come out of me. Now.

I washed my hands and left the tap running. The noise of the running water would drown out the sound. I got down on my hands and knees in front of the dirty toilet bowl. It was like a ceremonial ritual every time—bowing down to the toilet. Piss had run down the sides of it and dried. Nobody had cleaned this washroom in weeks.

I pointed my index and middle finger and jammed them down my throat. I gagged and coughed, but the sound of the running water covered it up, I thought. I hoped. I jammed my fingers down my throat again, until the tips of my nails hit the top of my esophagus and could

not go down any further. Something was coming up. *This is good.*
The harder I could slam my fingers, the faster it would come up. But
sometimes if I jammed too fast and hard, the pain would make my
eyes water and get puffy and red. And then I'd have to douse my face
with cold water to get the swelling down, or else explain myself to
people when I got out of the bathroom: "No, I'm fine, just something
in my eye."

It took four hard shoves of my fingers before the first batch
finally came out. The vomit exploded out of my throat, past my teeth,
then splattered all over the toilet bowl.

Why does heaving sound like someone's being choked to death?

The vomit came out with so much force that water splashed back
at me. Toilet water on my forehead, like a baby being baptized; I'm
christened a mess.

Whenever I binged and then purged, I'd follow the sequence of
what I eaten backwards to make sure I got it all out. Some celebrity
said the same thing in her book. My doctor said that didn't make
sense—that when you start eating, the food churns all together and
digests as one big mixture—but I still needed to visually account for
everything I had eaten.

A line of puke-tinged saliva ran from my mouth to the water. I
saw the cheese, the chips, some vegetables from the nacho platter.
But I didn't see the chocolate or the smoked salmon, so I knew I had to
keep going. It was a good start, though. Maybe only four or five more
batches, and then I'd be good and empty. I should have had more pop.
Anything fizzy. Another rule: carbonation always made throwing up
easier.

I jammed my fingers down again, and then again. Finally, a
second batch came up, and I saw more of what I'd eaten. Brown
chunks—that was the chocolate. A sense of relief came over me. Just a
few more times, and I could stop and start cleaning myself up.

Puke has a sour, acidic smell, depending on what you've eaten, of course. I'd become too familiar with it. At first it disgusted me. Then I got used to it. Now it soothed me—its presence confirmed that I successfully rid myself of what I had shoved in.

"Are you almost done in there?" someone asked, banging on the door. I looked toward the sound in a panic. *Shit. Go away.* I wasn't done yet. I needed more time. If I didn't get it all out, I was going to get fat. *Go away.*

"Tony, is that you in there? You okay?" the voice continued.

"Lisa?" I asked.

"Yeah. Hurry up. I gotta go, hon."

"Just give me two minutes."

Fuck fuck fuck.

I only puked twice. I didn't get everything out.

I stood up and washed my hands as fast as I could. Then I looked in the mirror: vomit dripping from the sides of my face. I ran my face under the cold water, hoping to get the vomit off and stop the swelling at the same time. I wet some toilet paper under the water, wiped down the inside of toilet and then flushed. But the room still reeked. I opened the medicine cabinet and found some ladies' perfume—one of the Chanel's, I think it was No. 5—and spritzed in a circular motion. Okay, I figured I'd cleared all the evidence.

"You okay?" Lisa asked as I opened the door. She glared at me.

"Fine." I tried to avoid making eye contact with her. "Just feeling a little sick. I think I'm gonna head out. I'll text you." I walked away before she could reply. I left the party without saying goodbye to anyone.

I drove home like a madman. I never let a binge sit inside of me for more than an hour. If I waited any longer, I worried that I'd start digesting it and turn it into fat. I never binged far from home, so I'd never be forced to use a washroom that wasn't my own. I'd broken that rule tonight.

I ran straight to my bathroom, determined to get the rest of the food out. It comforted me to be in my own bathroom. It was familiar. I shoved my fingers down my throat, harder than ever, so much that blood came up as I puked. I kept going. I had to make up for lost time. Thirty minutes later, most of the food—along with my anxiety—was gone; I believed I had got every last morsel out of my system. I washed myself up, cleaned the bathroom, and went to the kitchen. I always had Ziplocs of ice in the freezer for after an episode. I pulled a couple bags out and pressed them to my red, swollen cheeks. I grabbed my water bottle and went to the bedroom, where I downed two Paxils, three imipramines, one bromazepam, one Imovane, five fat burners and two laxatives.

I had pressed the restart button. It was like this night had never happened, like so many nights before.

I climbed into bed and pressed the ice bags to my face again. I shut my eyes.

Chapter 3: Thud

I had this recurring dream about my mother.

It always began with a line of people that reached from the front doors of my childhood church, ran through the centre aisle between the pews and ended in front of the altar. The people in the line, mostly my family and friends, would respectfully step aside as I walked down the aisle, dressed in my best suit from Sears and holding a bouquet of roses. It could have been a wedding, only there was one person short of a couple.

My mom's coffin lay at the front of the church. It was made of dark cherry wood with a shiny finish and silk lining. That part was true to life. Her whole life she had prided herself on appearing to have the best of everything: a beautiful house, a reputable job, brand-name clothes, a perfect son and so on. She always said she wanted to achieve the Western dream. When she first moved to Canada from the Philippines in the '70s, she spent a year taking English classes to rid herself of her accent, and she frequently used skin-bleaching creams to try to lighten her skin. She'd often pinch my nose, or tell me to pinch my nose, because it was "too Asian, too wide."

In the dream, I would make my way to the open casket. Mother was always wearing an ivory dress with embroidery on the sleeves and bodice. Her face didn't resemble her. It looked stretched. I reached down to touch her arm—her skin felt like cold paper. I would kneel and place the bouquet of roses in her stiff hands, close my welling eyes and begin reciting a prayer, just like she and I had done on many Sunday evenings.

A breeze would brush my face, and the crowd would gasp. I'd open my eyes to Mother sitting up in the coffin, glaring at me with displeasure. Then her voice: as loud and as disciplinary as when I was younger and I brought home a test mark lower than an A+: "Tony, stop crying ... And don't kill my roses!" She would toss the bouquet of flowers in my face, and hastily drop back in her coffin. Thud.

That was where the dream always ended, and I'd wake up in a sweaty panic.

It greeted me every few months. I'd had it for sixteen years, since I was eighteen—when my mother actually died. The events of the dream were real, with the exception of her rising from the dead to scold me.

In 1999, a lump formed in the middle of her chest. On the day of her biopsy, I waited in the hospital hallway while she got her results in the doctor's office. The door opened, and she walked out without looking at me. I went into the office where the doctor confirmed the news; I cried as I walked back to the car where my mom was waiting for me. The car ride was silent except for the sound of me sniffling and blowing my nose.

Why is this happening to her? To us? I wondered. *We're both good people. We go to church and pray to God. We don't deserve this.*

We drove for what seemed forever. Eight months later I was at the church, kneeling in front her corpse.

My mother and I were close. Dad left when I was six. "You're my only guy," she would often say to me.

Her words from the dream never left my mind: "Don't kill my roses!" My mom was a was a talented gardener who left behind a sea of red roses in our backyard. She always said that after she was gone, I'd surely kill them by underwatering or some other sort of negligence.

Of course, my neurosis could not accept the dream at its cursory level. I had psychoanalyzed her words and concluded that the garden had represented the blossoming future she had created for me. She had done so much for me and didn't want me to fuck it up. I was right. She *did* do everything for me. She worked two jobs to save for my tuition and buy a nice detached house. She tried to help me with my homework so I could be the smartest kid in class. She would not let being a single mother get in the way of making me a success. More often than not, I felt like her driving me to succeed was the ultimate middle finger to my father: "Look asshole, I raised this genius all on my own!" She never said that out loud, but I could see her vengeance. When she died, I felt the weight of her expectations. If I was a failure, then so was she. Or so thought my last psychiatrist.

My mom and I bonded over our love of romantic comedies, books, poetry, and fashion. The dress she was buried in was one of the last decisions we made together. As she got sicker, I felt it necessary to give her the chance to at least choose the dress for her grand entrance to the afterlife. I showed her three different outfits while she lay in her bed. But I couldn't ask the question. I couldn't say it out loud. So I mumbled something more vague: "Which dress do you like the most, Mom?" She slowly focused her gaze on one of them. Although she was only somewhat coherent, I felt like she knew what I was really asking: "Which dress do you want to be wearing when you're dead, Mom? Shall we go with the ivory?"

I knew she knew deep down that I was gay; how could she not, with the aforementioned stereotypical evidence? But I could never gather the courage to tell her, even though I'd known I liked boys since I was eleven.

"If you have something to tell your mother, now would be the time to say it," Barb, the nurse said two weeks before Mom died. I was conflicted: at times I felt the urgency of the situation and wanted to spill everything. But my mother was a devout Catholic; the only man in her life since my dad had been God. So I'd stop myself. If I told her I liked boys, she would have dropped dead of shame right then and there. "What?! I raised a gay, a homosexual?! A bakla ("gay" in Tagolog)?!" Thud.

I missed her. It would have been nice to know her as an adult. I'd have liked to think she would have been fine with other people thinking her son was a "nice guy."

Monday at 6:00 a.m. my alarm went off. Like I did every weekday, I hit the snooze button till 7:00, then headed to work at Melo and Company at Yonge and Wellington with a pasted-on smile, reciting the requisite courtesy hellos before parking myself at my cubicle for the day.

After Ken moved out, I couldn't afford to keep paying the mortgage on my mother's house. Her insurance payout had been minimal, and teaching creative writing at Gold's Community Arts Centre only paid $10.25 an hour. So in September of 2010, I dropped to teaching part-time Monday and Wednesday nights plus weekends, and got a full-time office job. Melo and Co. was a marketing and consulting firm that helped businesses sell their products or operate more efficiently. I started as a receptionist earning minimum wage without benefits. Within six months, I was promoted to assistant making $12.50 per hour, and two years later I was made an operations coordinator making $2.00 more. By 2012, my annual salary had increased to $26,000 and I finally had benefits. But through all my changing job titles and duties, one thing remained steady: I was a high performing cubicle daydreamer; despite any work task, I excelled in ruminating on anything and everything I felt didn't go my way in life, and what could have/should have/would have been if say, both my parents stuck around, or if Ken stayed with me, and so on and so on. Unfortunately, that was not part of my annual performance reviews.

I saw Melo and Co. struggle during more volatile market periods, and break even during stable ones. We had been in the red in recent years, prompting a salary freeze that had been in place since 2013. Having seen some of my coworkers get let go due to "business restructuring," I was just happy to have a job. I also knew that my lack of a degree would hinder my chances at more profitable positions at more lucrative and stable companies. Having been there for five years, most people assumed I was going to be a lifer.

On this particular day, I saw my boss, Victor Melo—whom I referred to as "Jell-O"—telling jokes at the water cooler while Lauren, the new intern, laughed at his every word. Yes, Jell-O was overweight. But I wasn't one to judge people on this issue. Actually, I was the very last person to judge someone on it. Still, I couldn't help the nickname. Whatever got me through the day.

Jell-O was one of those business men who'd walk past you in the hallway and do a fake gun shot with his hand and say, "How's it going, big guy?" in a voice that sounded like it belonged on the radio. He'd often tell politically incorrect or just plain unfunny jokes and then laugh at them out loud. He used a lot of corporate-speak, like "Let's think outside the box," "We're having great synergy on this," "Let's not reinvent the wheel," "Do we have any numbers on that?" and "What are our best practices here?" Sometimes my coworkers and I played buzzword bingo, counting how many times Jell-O said each of his pet phrases in a day or a given meeting. He spewed them out at any opportunity. He always had to have the last snappy word or catchy phrase in a discussion, and then would make a dramatic exit.

He waltzed into my cubicle with his familiar smirk.

"Tony-Tone," he said.

"Yes?" I answered.

"How's it going, big guy?"

"It's goo—"

"So what are your thoughts on the EFT account? What's the ETA on that?" Jell-O loved interrupting people by asking rapid questions.

"I thought you said you wanted to take the lead on that?"

"But I didn't want to take the glory away from you, Tony-Tone. What have you come up with so far?"

I grabbed my notepad and fumbled through the pages. Jell-O started to make sniffing noises.

"What's that smell?"

"Smell?" I felt uneasy.

"It smells like puke or something. You don't smell that?"

"Oh. Maybe. I'm not sure. Maybe the cleaning lady didn't change the garbage." I tried to be nonchalant.

I kept riffling through my note pad and found the account. "So. EFT Enterprises ... They seem to be having an issue with their invoicing process so—"

"Continue." He was always interrupting for no reason.

"Anyway, it seems like there are too many applications in their process. If we can get developers of the main software to allow for—"

"Tony!"

"Yes?"

"I'm just gonna stop you right there."

"Okay..."

"What's the main strategy for our clients here at Melo?"

I paused. I knew this bit. He liked to say it quite loudly, so it could be heard beyond my cubicle walls.

The main strategy we'd recommend for businesses that approached us was to "quantify and cut"; account for the time each procedure took, and if that procedure took too long, then cut. Account for the dollars spent, then cut. Account for the amount of people working and earning a living, and cut.

I began to respond. "Quanti—"

He jumped in: "Quantify and cut, Tone. Quantify and cut … say it, Tony."

"Quantify and cut."

"Bingo," Jell-O said, giddy like a kid.

"Yes," I said. "So, like I was saying, I quantified the inputting procedure, then timed and quantified the accounting team's process, and then exported the data into this spreadsheet, which calculates the average timings."

"Yes, quantify!" Jell-O repeated.

"We can save time in their process by eliminating the—"

"Eliminate?" he asked.

"Cut. I mean cut." *Cut cut cut, for fuck's sake.*

"Yes, go on." The excitement in his voice was rising.

"We can save time in their process by cutting the accounting team's software and having them just do the audit checks on the existing application, provided the developers can create that process. That'll take at least five minutes off each file. Quantify and cut."

"Why don't we just cut the accounting process out of it completely?" Jell-O asked.

"We can't do that. That's a required process."

"I think we should just cut it."

"I'm not sure, Victor."

"Well, whatever. But that's a great concept, Tone. Cutting the accounting process, I mean. You know, trimming the fat! I love it! We'll present it at our meeting next Monday."

"But—"

He left the cubicle and went back to the water cooler. I heard Lauren-the-intern laughing at his jokes again.

Just hold it all in. Don't say anything. Swallow it and hold it all in.

Whenever I got frustrated or overwhelmed, or if I made a mistake, he'd pull me into a meeting room for a pep talk. He loved giving platitude-filled pep talks. As he paced back and forth in front of me, I'd stare at his stomach. *I may be incompetent, but at least I'm not fat,* I'd think. It was horrible, but the best way I could cope.

At 5:05 p.m. I ran out of the office to catch the subway to the arts centre. Gold's was at Bloor and Spadina, only a fifteen-minute subway ride from Melo, so I had some time to snooze and reset myself before getting in front of the kids. I'd often thought about quitting the teaching job, but in addition to needing the money, I loved being with the kids too much. They reminded me of myself when I was thirteen and took a writing class there, hoping to create a masterpiece.
Now I got to see other children chase the same dream. The look of possibility—of hope—on the children's faces was endearing, even if I knew their dreams were unlikely to come true. And at the end of the month, I could stay afloat, even if only the tip of my nose was above the water's surface.

Chapter 5: Muzzle

"Nice to meet you, Tony," Dr. Tee said, grasping my hand. "Your hands are cold."

The examination room was freezing. Dr. Tee looked down and scanned my file. "Just one minute."

What does my file say? What is he thinking about me?

"You were seeing Dr. Abdi up near Rosehill for the last year. Why did you decide to switch?"

"I wasn't really benefiting from the sessions."

"Why not?"

"I just found he talked too much in clichés. Platitudes. A lot of the advice he gave was common sense. "

"Okay. Why don't you tell me why you think you need a psychiatrist?"

"I've had depression and anxiety since I was a teenager. It started after my mom died. I'm on a few different meds. I think they help. I don't feel sad. But I don't really feel happy either. I guess feeling nothing is better than feeling sad."

"I can imagine." Dr. Tee shuffled through my file again. "So currently you are on sixty milligrams a day of paroxetine for anxiety, thirty milligrams of imipramine for depression, plus one milligram of bromazepam to calm you down as needed and 7.5 milligrams of

Imovane for sleep. Is that all of them?"

"Yeah."

"And according to your file, you used to be on Wellbutrin?"

"Yes, but that gave me nightmares."

"And for a while, Effexor?"

"Yeah, but that gave me dry mouth. And I was still anxious and depressed."

"You also tried Celexa?"

"Yup. Didn't work either."

"Would you want to try other ones? Zoloft… Prozac maybe?"

"I don't think I'm up for trying anything new. The process is exhausting."

"Fair enough. We can always revisit it later."

"How about your physical health?" Dr. Tee scanned my body. "Are you eating okay? You look gaunt. Any issues there?"

I couldn't tell him. I couldn't even say the words—eating disorder—out loud. "No. I'm fine."

"You sure?"

I couldn't tell him.

I couldn't tell him that yesterday morning, I was craving toast—not with avocado like those silly millennials—but with the good stuff: Nutella. Or condensed milk. Even plain old butter with piles of sugar on top.

I couldn't tell Dr. Tee that I didn't have toast yesterday because I didn't have a toaster. I had thrown it out after my thirtieth birthday. That was to stop those kinds of moments: the sudden cravings for food, specifically for the c-word. No, not that one. The other c-word, the one that spooks gay men even more: carbohydrates. All that food we crave and love, which loves us back by latching onto our stomach, hips, face and ass. So, I threw away the toaster and the starvation began. And once I got used to suppressing those cravings and hunger pains, they started to fade away.

I couldn't tell Dr. Tee that my craving to be thin was stronger than my craving for toast yesterday. That when I was eighteen, my five-foot-0.75-inch frame weighed in at 140 pounds, and I'd had to carefully select my clothes to hide my pudgy frame. Once my mom pinched my chest and said, "You have suso, Tony." Suso means breasts in Tagalog. "Be careful you don't turn into a woman." She just giggled, thinking it was harmless.

I couldn't tell him that I was a different kind of gay man back then. I was stuck in the closet, all the while wanting to burn the clothes in there because they were meant for someone much bigger than me. I wanted to say it was my mother's fault, but then I'd be one of those cliché therapy patients who blamed everything on their parents. If I lost even a bit of weight, my mother would get upset— saying "Why are you losing weight? People will think I'm not feeding you. So eat!"—ironically adding to the problem that gave me my "suso."

I couldn't tell Dr. Tee that throughout my twenties I'd thought about my weight a lot, trying the odd diet and exercise craze, and that the breakup with Ken had escalated those efforts into a full-scale battle over the last five years: the battle against those forty pounds of my unwanted self.

Quantify, cut.

That I joined a gym in October 2010 and did an hour of cardio, four days a week. Ten pounds melted quickly, much to my delight. I then cut my meal portions in half. In December of that year, I cut out carbs completely. Being Asian, I felt very strange not having rice. Meals were incomplete, and I was hungry... empty. As if losing the rice—and, in turn, the weight—meant losing my "yellowness." But another twenty pounds dropped away. By the spring of 2011, I'd cut out dinner completely. *Quantify, cut.* By fall, I wanted to cut my wrists. But I thought, *Will that help me get thinner? Probably not.* So bleeding to death wasn't an option. By the end of 2011, I was at 98 pounds. Instead of food, I fed off compliments: "You've lost so much weight, you look amazing!", "Holy shit, you look like a different person!", "What is your secret?" If I tipped the scale into triple digits, I'd starve myself and deal with the hunger pains by taking naps and/or going to sleep early. I was weak, and always cold, but at least I knew that people would be jealous of my size-26 jeans. Someone would be envious of *me*.

I couldn't tell him that every day was a practice in planning out my calorie consumption. In the morning, I had half a granola bar and a large coffee with milk and seven Splenda sweeteners. Yes, seven. I never had real sugar for fear of the calories. I probably wouldn't have known what it tasted like anymore. It was really my only treat so I figured I should go all out. It soon became an addiction—I had to carry Splenda packets everywhere I went and discreetly add it to food or drinks when people weren't looking. Not that people would care to see me fumble with white powder anyway. The sweetness gave me a high; I may as well have pulled out a mirror and snorted lines of that shit.

Breakfast was about a hundred calories. Then for lunch, I'd have a small salad with a can of tuna and some low-fat dressing. Another four hundred calories. Ten grams of carbohydrates. And then no dinner. If I felt lightheaded, I'd just have another coffee. On the days that I had a social outing, such as dinner with friends, I'd skip the breakfast granola bar and just have the coffee, skip the lunch, and then just order a salad at dinner. I could not go over 500 calories for the day or my anxiety would spin out of control. No spontaneous meals—every bit of food was planned in advance.

I couldn't tell him that even after losing all that weight, I still went to the gym on the nights I didn't teach and did cardio for forty-five minutes. I lifted light weights for a while, but as I lost more and more weight, even that required too much strength; I had to reserve my energy for not fainting on the way home. I'd go immediately to bed to avoid being awake and feeling the hunger pains. Night was my favourite part of the day—my hunger was temporarily alleviated by my daily medications; my consciousness temporarily alleviated by slumber.

I couldn't tell Dr. Tee that in addition to the paroxetine, imipramine, bromazepam and Imovane, I started taking fat burners, laxatives and diuretics. The day that I found out that Ex-lax made laxatives in chocolate form, I felt like a kid getting a pony for his birthday.

I couldn't tell him that trying to function on nothing started to take its toll. I felt hungry, cold and tired all the time. If I got out of bed too quickly, or stood up from my chair after sitting for too long, my vision would fade to black. My cuticles were ripped and my gums bled. I'd wake up to find my hair on the pillow; it had fallen out while I slept. But then these were side effects of an eating disorder, so I'd be comforted by the suffering: my efforts were working.

I couldn't tell him that all my childhood and teen years I'd been trapped in a closet, only to come out at nineteen and enter another kind of prison.

I couldn't tell him that my quarter-life crisis had generously extended itself into the next decade.

I couldn't tell him that all this had led to another problem. Because if I did, I'd have to tell him what that problem was.

I couldn't tell Dr. Tee anything. Shame was a muzzle that I couldn't get off of me.

On Thursday, I rushed out of the Melo office to Le Jardin near the gay village to meet my friends Nick and Lisa. Jell-O wanted more revisions on the EFT project, so I'd ended up working late and almost forgetting about my dinner with them. Luckily, it was within walking distance.

Whenever I walked through the underground of the financial district, I noticed an increasing presence of young gay men. "Guppies" (a combination of "gay" and "yuppy"), or "A-Gays," as they were often called, were barely out of university, wore suits that fit like spandex over their perfectly toned or overly muscled bodies, Prada shoes, and had their hair gelled so tightly back that it must've been hard for them to blink. They were accessorized to the extreme, with vibrant ties that matched their socks, which accented their leather shoulder bags, which matched their shoes and belts. And on top of all that, they would all have same red and black gym bag from GoodLife.

They were like Ken dolls.

They'd be huddled in circles at the Starbucks or at village bars after work, gossiping with each other about office drama, and complaining about how everyone else at work was completely incompetent. The self-congratulatory tales of their contributions to work projects were like status masturbation: "That place would fall apart without me! I should have been promoted to director ages ago!" And if you talked to a Guppy or A-Gay and their occupation came up, without fail the word "professional" would precede their glorified job title: "I'm a professional coordinator" … "I'm a professional business consultant" … "I'm a professional executive administrative assistant." I heard that last one from a twenty-two-year-old at one of the bars. I wanted to say "relax … you're an office bitch, just like the rest of us." But that would've been mean.

The A-Gays were multiplying, and they'd gotten younger and younger since I started my career.

Why did this bother me?

Perhaps because I felt they were superficial and basic. Like I was better than them. Or, probably, I was jealous because they were handsome and confident with their best years seemingly ahead of them. And happy and hopeful. They seemed happy and hopeful for the future.

What was their secret to such a ridiculous notion?

Maybe they bothered me because they seemed more successful than I was, despite being ten or more years my junior. They didn't deserve their success because they hadn't suffered through that moment when age forces you to come face-to-face with one rather sad reality: life will disappoint you.

Maybe I was bitter because I thought that moment might not come for them at all.

Nick and Lisa were my best friends. I didn't have siblings; they were my surrogate family who pulled me through the mud after my mother died. I'd known Nick since grade school and had had a crush on him since we first met. He was tall, muscular, and stereotypically "masculine." He always played on all the sports teams in school. He was good looking, with a square jaw and bright eyes. If I didn't love him, I'd hate him. By seeming to be straight, he was the gay man every gay man wanted, and wanted to be.

When I told him I was gay when we were thirteen, he was blasé about it: "I know," he said, nodding. "So am I."

I was shocked. I had no idea. Then followed my confession: "I, um, kind of like, love you, like really. Like more than a friend."

Maybe he felt the same way about me, I thought. I hoped. Maybe I'll be the exception and he'll see something special in me. Like a rom-com right off the Lifetime channel.

"I know that too." He then looked into my eyes, smiled at me warmly, kissed me on the forehead, and tucked me under his arm. With that, I knew exactly what he was telling me: we were not going to live out that movie.

To say that Nick had an active sex life was an understatement. After college, he moved to Chatham for work, but within a year, he moved back to Toronto. He said he had slept with every guy in Southwestern Ontario and wanted to have a wide demographic again. Whenever he turned on his Grindr, his phone sounded like a pinball machine. Oddly, he'd had a boyfriend named Lucas for the last three years and they lived happily in an open relationship, something I'd never understood.

I met Lisa through Nick. She used to work in the data-entry office of the construction company he worked for. She was straight and single. She had put herself out on every dating app but never seemed to find anyone she liked. Her online chatting experiences all had a similar pattern: a guy messages her, she replies, they exchange two or three generic messages and then, randomly, the guy sends a photo of his penis.

"No logical or gradual lead-in ... just BAM, dick pic!" she'd say.

Despite their constant bickering, I thought Lisa had a crush on Nick too. I'd catch her staring at him with the same look of longing that I felt.

As I sat myself at the table, Nick was finishing up a phone call.

"It was huge bro. At least eight. Anyway, I'll tell you more later, gotta go. Later man." He hung up.

Lisa always greeted me with a hug and air kisses.

"How are you?" she said.

"Good."

Nick got up and put his closed fist out for me to bump with mine. I was always confused when he did that.

"Oh, shit, sorry. I was with straight people earlier." He took his fist back and gave me a hug. "Hey, brother."

"I was worried about you," Lisa said. "I hadn't heard from you since Rob's party last week. You just ran out of there. Didn't even say bye."

"Yeah, I was feeling sick," I said.

"I know. You ran like you'd committed a crime".

"Sorry, I wasn't feeling well."

"Bullshit!" Nick said. "You've been running outta parties all the time lately."

Shit. Do they know?

I tried to divert.

"Well, I don't know what we were doing there, Nick. Rob is your friend and he's like how old? Twenty-one?"

Nick smirked. "He's twenty-three, okay? So what? He's hot. I'd take that in any hole in my body… and you both know I ain't no bottom!"

I rolled my eyes. "Yes, yes, you're not a bottom. Anyway, we're too old to be babysitting your flavour of the month."

Lisa chuckled.

"You're just being cynical, Tony. You used to be so much fun," Nick said. "Anyway, how's work?"

"Same."

"Oh no. What'd your boss do now?" Lisa asked.

"Oh same thing, you know."

"You know you're gonna have to tell him off one day."

I nodded. "Yeah I know. I just have to pick my battles. If I complained about everything, I wouldn't get any work done. What'd you guys do last night?"

Lisa rolled her eyes. "I was at work till eight."

"Again?" asked Nick.

"Yeah." She shook her head. "I work through my lunch and stay late every day now. And they're gonna offshore another bunch of jobs, so everybody is working their asses off because they're scared shitless. We're robots running on fear."

"Sorry," I said.

"It gets better," she said. "So yesterday, my boss comes and tells me that my contract is ending in like a month. I'm like "yes, I know." He tells me that they aren't renewing my contract due to the headcount, and that I can reapply in September and there's a good chance I'll get hired back. But then this woman from another department who's been there for seven years said they do that so they don't have to make you permanent and give you benefits. That's their way of getting around it. Fucking ridiculous."

"What the fuck?" Nick said. "You guys need to get away from your desk jobs. Get into construction with me. Houses will always need to be built."

"Yeah, but who can afford to buy houses now? Can you afford a new house, Tony?" Lisa asked. "That 20% down payment is only like, what, eighty grand?"

"Nope. Not on my salary," I said.

"Dude, you're working two jobs," Nick said.

"Yeah, and that's just to get by."

"You don't have anything saved?"

Just hold it all in. Don't get mad.

I couldn't. Nick was one of my best friends, but it angered me that he could just assume my financial situation could easily be fixed.

"Do *you*? Wanna fuckin' pay for my down payment there,

Daddy?" I snapped.

A waiter approached. Nick smirked at the waiter, looking him up and down.

"Hey guys, all ready to order?"

"The veal."

"Just a burger for me."

My turn. *Shit.*

"You know what, I had a huge lunch. I'll just get a green tea," I said.

The waiter left. I saw Lisa give Nick a look.

"What?" I said defensively.

"Green tea?" she said.

I turned to Nick. "So what'd you do last night?"

"I went to the spa."

The spa was another word for bathhouse. Bones on Church Street was the one where the "hot" guys went. If you were brown or Asian and didn't want to be invisible, you'd go to Senses a few streets over.

"You still go?" Lisa asked.

"Yeah. But I think I like online better," Nick said. "It's so hard now to reject people at the bathhouse in person when you can just swipe left online. I feel so cruel. But then again at Bones, you get to see what people actually look like without photoshop. Ha!"

"I don't know how you and Lucas do it," I said.

"Do what?"

"Be in an open relationship."

"Dude, after being with someone for three years, you have to. You can't just fuck the same dude over and over. Can you eat the same meal every single day? No."

"Well, Tony does," Lisa said.

"What?"

"You eat a salad every day. Don't think we don't notice."

"I do not."

"Anyway," Nick said. "That's how modern love works now. You just have to let it go ... and then go with it. You know, some yin-yang shit."

I didn't understand that. I mean, I understood open relationships, but I could never do it.

"Oh yeah, that reminds me—it's Lucas's birthday party next Friday. The Meat Locker. You guys are coming."

"Sure," Lisa said.

Nick looked at me. "You're coming. No is not an option. You can't flop out again!"

"Okay," I said.

I was exhausted and had terrible hunger pains. I'd also developed a huge canker sore inside my left cheek, causing a sharp, pulsing sting. I got canker sores a lot. WebMD said they could be caused by stress and poor diet.

I watched in a daze as Nick scarfed down his veal and Lisa chewed her burger. At one point, it seemed the grease on their plates caught the light and sparkled, blinding my eyes, and I lost track of the conversation. It was like a romance, the food causing a twinkle in my eye.

They were always on me about my lack of focus when I was out with them, saying that I was always lost or confused about the topic of discussion. Or that I was short and rude with them. Or didn't respond to their questions. I wasn't present, they said. But when I was hungry, life moved in slow motion. It took longer for me to receive information, process it, and then scrape together a reply.

I was upset with myself too—I'd forgotten that I was meeting them for dinner. Had I remembered, I wouldn't have eaten that salad for lunch at my desk. I would have saved the calories for Le Jardin. To Lisa and Nick, I'd look like a normal person eating a meal, but to me, eating at a nice restaurant would have been my reward for starving myself all day.

The last time I had been to Le Jardin was in the fall of 2010, shortly after I started my job at Melo. Getting used to my new surroundings was stressful. After dinner with Lisa and Nick—at which I'd hastily scarfed down a salad—I went to the Dufferin Mall to eat more. I did that often—eat small in public, then more in private. I'd stuff myself, then feel guilty, then not eat for days and then go back to calorie restriction.

My first stop was McDonald's: a Big Mac combo. With a milkshake. Then I went to Manchu Wok for dumplings and noodles, then to Cinnabon, and then finally Dairy Queen. I could feel my stomach expanding and tightening, but the taste of the food overwhelmed me, and I couldn't stop. With each bite, I could feel myself salivating and my eyes rolling back. My belly was so full I could barely breathe.

When I got home that night, the pain in my stomach was unbearable. The regret was worse.

I'd once read an article about some celebrity's battle with bulimia. She said she'd stick a toothbrush down her throat to get the food up. The idea had always intrigued me, but I was a bit scared. I was terrified of hurting myself, ripping my esophagus or something. But I was in so much discomfort that evening that I pushed away my fear. I picked up my toothbrush and lightly poked it down my throat. Nothing happened. I tried a few more teases, and still nothing. I realized I'd have to be braver and more forceful if I wanted the food out of me.

Fuck, just do it. Don't be such a pussy.

I put the toothbrush down and jammed two fingers down my throat with so much force that I gagged and coughed. My eyes watered. *Just do it.* I took a deep breath and did it again, and this time vomit rushed up my throat and exploded into the toilet.

Holy shit. I just did it. I hit the magic button.

Something I'd pressed deep in my throat had miraculously pulled everything up from my stomach. It was like hitting control-Z on the computer. The refund button at the cash register. Undo what I just did, pretend it never happened. I did it again and again until the bowl was filled with vomit. With the tension in my stomach fading, the high feeling in my head got stronger. When I was done, a revelation had come over me: if I did this all the time, I would never get fat. I could eat what I wanted, as much as I could dream of, and get away with it. Never suffer the consequences.

Overspend; return it. Send the wrong email; recall it. Mess up your document; control-Z. Stuff your face; throw it up. The undo button. The eraser. The morning-after pill. So many ways to make things disappear, like they never happened, no traces. No responsibility taken.

Since that day, I had committed myself to this cycle of calorie restriction, then bingeing, then purging, then back to calorie restriction. For the most part, I felt like I had accomplished my goal. Seeing the shadows of my cheekbones, or eight of my ribs protruding from my sides, gave me immense satisfaction. Every now and then, I even thought I looked good.

But then there were times when I looked at other guys—posing at the village bars, or networking at the coffee shops—and my mind was consumed with envy. There were countless perfect Ken dolls out there who didn't seem to give a shit about their appearance. They smoked, drank and ignored the gym. They ate bread and sweets without remorse— they even photographed it and posted it on their Instagram as if to say, "Look at me, I ate this, therefore I am fabulous!" How could they do that? And yet I knew they would always look better than me. Those meatheads at the office, the perky twinks in H&M, the millennials on Queen West. If those guys tried as hard as I did and actually cared about their appearance, they'd be on the cover of GQ. Meanwhile, I would never be more than average. Perhaps cute, at best. And no one wants to fuck cute.

I tried to tell myself to accept how the real world worked. But it hurt. Relying on my personality was simply not working, at least it hadn't with Ken. Since our breakup, I'd become a jaded and bitter Barbie. But what I had discovered after that trip to the Dufferin Mall food court—bingeing and purging—was that I *could* cope with it all. I didn't have to worry about what food and how much of it I put inside me, because it would just be coming out later. And that was a relief. As the years went by, it got even easier to let out the vomit; at the same time, it got harder to say the words that needed to come out: *I need help.*

Chapter 7: Great Whites

The following Monday was the day of our meeting with EFT Enterprises. Lauren-the-intern told me that the clients were in the lobby.

"Matt Green. Nice to meet you," the white man said, shaking my hand.

"I'm Tony."

There was an Asian man with him. "Sunny Wang," he said, extending his hand.

"Great," I said, "follow me. Victor is in the meeting room."

We walked down the hallway. I hated having people walk behind me. I worried that they'd stare at my butt and the bald spot at the back of my head.

"Pardon the mess," I said, as we passed some drywall marked with caution tape. "We're doing some renovations."

The cubicle walls in the office were being removed; we would soon be working in a "cafeteria-style" office, with all desks set up in rows. They said it was to encourage collaboration, but I thought it was to eliminate physical barriers for people to hide behind. A clear line of sight across the battlefield.

Employees would no longer have a permanent work station; they would have to find a new desk to work at every day. No personal items would be permitted at each station, and we'd have to bring all of our belongings to and from a personal storage cabinet every day. I had a photo of my mother and me at a family wedding in the Philippines up on my wall, but HR told me I'd have to take it down. I liked having people see it. I was pretty hefty in those days; people were always shocked that it was me in the photo, and they showered me with compliments about how great I looked after losing all that weight.

The elimination of the staff's personal items, in addition to the removal of decorations in the lunch room, hallways, and meeting rooms and a reduction in printing on paper, was being called a "digital renovation." Less physical, more virtual. Accordingly, we heard a rumour that the staff would be literally reduced or replaced by offshore contract workers if necessary to ration financial resources. We would need to be a more flexible workforce, contingent upon business needs.

Quantify, cut.

Even words were being cut. An email had come out, informing us all that from then on, communications were to be "as brief as possible," and to "please refrain from including any unnecessary words or phrases." This was surely a way to justify Jell-O's habit of never fully reading emails; he ignored any correspondence that had more than two sentences. "If possible, Tones, just write the gist of the message in the subject line," he would tell me. Words had become meaningless, so might as well eliminate them at any opportunity.

Matt and Sunny scanned the environment as we walked past the grey maze of identically sterile cubicle squares. "Nice office you have here," Matt said. I just nodded; I didn't feel like making small talk. The only sounds after that were the frantic tapping on keyboards and the clicking of mice. During the stressful busy season, one wouldn't hear people talking about the increased workload; only the sounds of more intense typing and clicking, faster and louder.

Many of our clients—including Matt—were older white

businessmen with grey hair and grey suits, and they blended in perfectly with our endless bare grey-and-white walls. Grey-and-white businessmen, floating around the office like sharks, their smiling mouths open, showing their sharp, shiny teeth, their round bodies camouflaged until you happened to notice that your head had been bitten off.

Matt was the owner of EFT and Sunny the director of finance. I never felt like job titles meant anything, but it was nice to see an Asian man like Sunny in a position that suggested some sort of authority.

Jell-O liked to talk in generalities when laying out business proposals. Whenever he felt clients were beginning to see how little he understood, he'd pull out a catchy phrase like, "let's hit the ground running," or "this is our hands-on approach," or "Tony, let's run the numbers on that offline." That last phrase was code for "Tony, I have no idea what the fuck I'm talking about, so take over now." It became a whole song and dance—same speech, same jokes, same handshake.

Despite my warning, Jell-O suggested eliminating the accounting verification stage from EFT's procedures: "It's simple gentlemen. We quantify, then we cut."

Matt and Sunny weren't convinced. "Victor, that's a big process we need. How do we know everything will be accurate?" Green asked.

Jell-O's ability to keep a straight face in these instances always impressed me. "I understand the concern, Matt. I assure you, we haven't miscalculated. We're just trimming the fat here." He then hit the panic button and looked at me: "Tony, just for Matt, let's run the numbers on that offline again. Right away."

I'd known that line was coming; I was surprised it had taken Jell-O that long to say it.

"Sure," I said. "I'll have that for you all as soon as possible."

Chapter 8: No Femmes, No Fatties, No Fish

I found myself in Dr. Tee's office the next day, freezing yet again.

He asked me what I remembered from my mother's illness.

"I remember when I was eighteen and had just spoken with my mom's oncologist. He told me she would die within the next five months," I said.

"That must have been difficult to hear," Dr. Tee said.

"I started crying. It was hard to stop myself from doing it the rest of the day, and at work —I worked at a grocery store at the time—the supervisor asked me what was wrong. So I told her. She said, 'I'm so sorry to hear about your mom, Tony. But stop crying. Go wash your face. You are a man.' *You are a man.* I immediately stopped crying."

"And how did that make you feel?" Dr. Tee asked.

"I was mad! I'm sorry, what did she just say? I couldn't believe someone could be so insensitive. I wanted to tell her to fuck off and punch her in the face. I didn't, but would that have been an appropriate 'manly' response? Oh shit. Sorry for swearing."

"Don't worry about that."

I continued. "That was a long time ago, but what that stupid supervisor said and the idea of how to act like a man always stuck in my mind, especially when I came out of the closet."

"Interesting. Let's talk about that," Dr. Tee said.

Dr. Tee approached our session with a sense of looseness; he said he wasn't concerned if I started to rant and go off topic. He encouraged me to talk freely and wanted to see where my thoughts would lead us.

"Why do you think her comment bothered you so much?" he asked.

"I think it just messed with my head, the idea of being quote-unquote manly. Especially while being gay. Every now and then when I feel ballsy, I go online—mostly on Grindr—and it's obvious what guys are looking for: "masc for masc," "straight-acting only," "no femmes, no fatties, no fish.""

"No fish?"

"Code for no Asians."

"Terrible," Dr. Tee said, shaking his head.

"It's so confusing. According to Grindr and every other stupid app, to be a desirable gay man means you have to *not* act like you're gay—despite actually being gay—in addition to being fit and preferably white. Other than not being fat, I don't meet any of the criteria. Sometimes I wonder if that's why Ken dumped me. Did he just want the same thing as those Grindr profiles?"

Dr. Tee scribbled something on his notepad. "Don't stop talking, I'm listening, just jotting something down."

Ugh. He probably thought I was some bitter Barbie venting because I didn't feel special. I tried to lighten things up with a joke: "It made me feel better that profiles with those lines usually had spelling or grammatical errors. Who wants to be with someone stupid?"

Dr. Tee chuckled. *(Success!)*

"And don't get me started if on top of not being white, you were a bottom. You'd go right to the bottom of the gay un-lubed totem pole."

Dr. Tee laughed out loud this time. *(Success again!)* "Really?"

"I'm serious. If you aren't white, a top, over 5'10", very "manly" and straight-acting, fit, well-endowed and making over $80,000, you're on the bottom of this stupid hierarchy of douche-fags."

"That's pretty bleak. Do you think you might be a tad cynical?"

"No. There's this ideal we have to live up to and any variation from that is a no-no. Come on, you're Asian. You can empathize, no?"

"I don't know if this applies to straight people."

"Maybe it doesn't. Oh well, screw straight people." *Shit.* "Sorry. I sound like an ass."

"That's okay."

"Anyway, when you go to the bars on Church, all you hear is shit like, 'whoa that guy is fucking hot. Too bad he looks like he'd be a nelly bottom,' or, 'He was hot ... until he opened his mouth to talk and a purse flew out of his mouth, fucking queenie bottom.' You either hear, 'He was yellow ... but he was pretty hot,' or the reverse, 'he was really hot ... for an Asian.' It doesn't stop at Asians, either. 'Oh you like the chocolate? Ewww. I'm not a fan,' meaning black guys."

Dr. Tee shook his head.

"A friend of my friend Nick once said, 'I'm a top. I want a bottom. But no fucking feminine prissy type. I want a man. I am gay for God's sake. Did I mention I'm a top?' There's this preoccupation with every gay man to make sure that everybody knows he *isn't* a bottom. Is it because 'taking it' instead of 'giving it' means they'd be emasculated or less powerful? In a straight relationship, is the woman then reduced to being the 'bottom' of the relationship?"

My thoughts started running through my brain faster, and my mouth struggled to keep up: "Would I be right to assume that most gay men don't want to be thought of as bottoms because they don't want to be thought of as the 'woman?' Is homophobia—even internal—based on misogyny ... patriarchy? I was so pissed at Nick's friend. So I said, 'Did you say you were a top? I don't think I heard the first three times you said it.' He turned to Nick and said, 'your little friend is funny. What, Tony, you pissed cuz you a nelly bottom?'

So I said, 'that's right, my friend. Without us, what would you idiots wiggle your micro dicks into?' I didn't care if Nick would hate me for mouthing off to his friend. Then he said, 'I'd like to see you top something with that chopstick of yours buddy!' and walked away. Of course, along with bottom-shaming was underlying racism. I should have punched him too, like I wanted to punch my supervisor when I was eighteen. Was being violent 'manly'? If I started hitting people, would the line at bars then change to, 'you see that little Asian guy? He's a bottom, but fuck, he can throw a pretty good punch! Mad respect, man!'? If you're a bottom—and on top of that, not white— why is there an inherent assumption that you're less of a man unless you do something extra to prove otherwise?"

I paused. I was ranting like a lunatic.

"Oh my God, I'm sorry. I've totally gone off the rails."

"That's okay. Continue."

I sighed. "I can deal with homophobia within the straight world. But I refuse to deal with it in our own community. You would think that being gay and having faced all that hardship coming out would give you some perspective. Some fucking empathy."

Dr. Tee wrote on his notepad again, this time for more than a full minute. He then looked up and said, "Tony, I sense a lot of anger in you. And this is great—it's good to feel your emotions. But I think there maybe something more to it. Are you upset that you're in the minority and are getting the short end of the stick? Is it jealousy? The unfairness of it all?" He paused. "Or is there another problem underneath all this anger? You don't have to give me an answer right now. But just think about it."

I was afraid of what he was getting at.

"I'm just so...." I couldn't find the word.

"Mad? ...Helpless?... Jaded?" he said.

Suddenly, my stomach growled loud enough for both of us to hear. "Hungry," I said. "I'm just so hungry."

Dr. Tee chuckled.

"I apologize for my stomach," I said, smiling. "Gross."

Dr. Tee smiled warmly. "No need to apologize."

"How'd we do on Monday's homework? Do we like Haikus, guys?" I asked the class that Wednesday night.

"I don't," said Taylor.

"And why didn't we like it, Taylor?"

"It's too hard to keep counting all the syllables and write something pretty. It's harder than rhyming."

"It's just a stupid sentence cut up to fit a certain number of syllables," another student said.

"There's a discipline to it. That's what makes it beautiful," I said. I looked around. "Okay, who's next? John, how about you?"

John, a tall rumpled looking kid in glasses, stared at me and shook his head. "Mine's dumb."

"Blasphemy!" I said. "Go ahead."

He read his poem. "My beautiful son / Rise and shine like the bright sun / And cast into shadows, the mistakes of your father."

The class was quiet. Some of the kids who weren't paying attention perked their heads up.

"That was beautiful, John," I said. "Wow."

"I couldn't get it to fit into the right amount of syllables. Sorry."

"That's okay. Sometimes we need to ignore the rules to follow what means more to us."

I was slightly alarmed. This was the third time this boy had written something upsetting about his father. In week two, he wrote about how proud he was that he'd taught himself how to play basketball, because his dad wasn't around to do it. In week four, he wrote a passionate analysis about how Sylvia Plath's poem "Daddy" should be mandatory reading for all kids entering high school.

I approached him after class. I knew that look of sadness on his face, having lived it myself for so long.

"Hey, John. How are you liking the class so far?"

"I like it."

"Good."

"Good."

Through the slight opening of the classroom door I saw a young man looking inside the class, watching us. The hallway was poorly lit, but I was able to make out some loosely tossed curls. The handsome face flashed a big, beautiful smile.

I looked back at John.

"I don't want to get into your business here, but I can't help but notice that there's a theme in your writing, which is great. It gives you a personal stamp and distinguishes you from the crowd. But is there something on your mind, about, I don't know, your family? Your father? You want to talk about it?"

"No."

"You sure?"

"Yeah. It's just teenage angsty stuff. The usual."

"That doesn't mean it doesn't matter. Everybody's experience is unique to them."

"No, I'm fine. Thanks though."

"Okay. Well, anytime you want to swap stories, let me know. My dad is... you know ..." I didn't know how to phase it diplomatically. I tried again. "My dad provides ample material for my writing too."

John looked at me, puzzled.

"He can be a bit of dick," I said. John smiled.

That was a lie. I didn't know if my dad was a dick. I didn't know because I didn't know him at all.

"I gotta go," John said, grabbing his backpack and heading toward the door. "See you next class."

I looked up to the doorway and the handsome stranger was gone. I went out to the hallway. Maybe he was an older brother of one of the kids, I thought. Maybe he was one of the cleaners. I walked a ways down the hall toward the bathroom, but nobody was around.

Chapter 10: Antonio

It was Friday, the night of Lucas's birthday party. The party to which I promised Nick I would show up.

The Meat Locker was divided into three parts. Two were on the main floor—a bar overlooking a lounge area, and a dance floor on the other side of the room. At the back were spiral stairs that led up to the third part, known as the "locker" area, which was a pitch-black maze that had small enclosures where guys could get more private. I used to go to the club years ago, but had never had the courage to walk up to the lockers. Nick frequently went up there, and he often came back with crazy stories. Threesomes, gangbangs, drug exchange... after a while the stories got boring and blended into each other.

The last time I was there with Nick was for his twenty-fifth birthday. After that night, I swore I would never go back. After disappearing in the lockers for two hours—during which I was still too intimidated to go up there and look for him—Nick had come down completely dishevelled and stumbled into my arms. His hair, face and clothes were dripping.

"Why are you so wet?" I asked.

He didn't smell like alcohol. It was different. "What's that smell?"

He was obviously drunk and or high on something. "Dude, he asked me if I was into watersports."

"What?" I asked, slowly backing away from him.

"Yeah. He was so hot and so nice. He shared his drugs with me. So nice of him, right? So I was like, yeah sure, go for it," he said casually.

"Go for what?" I asked.

"He wanted to piss on me."

"What?!"

"Don't judge! It's all normal now. He was really respectful. If you loosened up, you'd have fun and not be so annoying," Nick said.

I'd sent Nick home in a cab, then rushed to the bathroom to wash my face and arms with extra hot water. Then I'd smeared on several of coats of hand sanitizer.

That was nine years ago. And here I was, back again.

The club was packed. You had to be nineteen to get into the club, but these boys looked younger. I felt like a pervert even looking at them.

The logistics of the scene hadn't changed. The disco strobe lights, the monotonous electronic beat, the boys trying to out-grind each other, the typical drunk boys, high and stumbling, their straight girlfriends indulging them. Then of course, the beautiful group of fit, white Ken dolls always walking through the dance floor, or leaning back against a pole, eyeing other perfectly chiseled, square-jawed white guys. Like sharks circling one another, waiting to bite—and make out. This bar, like all others, was another ocean scene starring the great whites, with all the non-square-jawed, non-Caucasians aimlessly floating at the top of the water, belly up.

As soon as I got there, I ran to the bathroom to check myself. I looked in the mirror and was happy to see that skipping my morning granola bar for the last three days had worked: my cheekbones were protruding, casting shadows down the sides of my face. I put my hands on my sides and felt the sharpness of my rib cage. I always made sure I could clearly see the outline of eight ribs whenever I got dressed.

You're going to be okay, I thought, reassuring myself. *You look skinny, you feel skinny. It's going to be a good night.* I had also taken eight fat burners an hour before heading out—yet another rule of mine—which absorbed any excess water I carried by the time I arrived at the event. I had to learn the hard way to take the caffeine-free ones; the first few times I took the regulars, I found myself in cold sweats and shaking like some addict, with my heart wanting to burst out of my chest. I knew the fat burners were working if my cheeks looked concave, and when I pissed, the urine would be three brighter shades of yellow. I edged myself away from the mirror and walked back to the bar.

As I made my way toward Nick and Lisa at the back near the stage, a tall, laughing hipster lost his balance and bumped into me. I swerved, and my left shoulder slammed against a large wooden column. He immediately rebalanced himself and walked back to his circle of friends, still laughing. He didn't even look at me.

Suddenly Nick appeared and tapped the guy on the shoulder. He said something I couldn't hear above the music. The hipster turned around and they both walked over to me.

"Sorry about that, man," he said. "Didn't see you."

"Thanks bro," Nick said. The guy walked back to his friends.

"Tone! I'm so happy you made it out!" Nick picked me up and spun us in circle.

"Well you gave me no choice," I said.

"Don't be a bitch," he replied with a smirk.

"I'm kidding. Of course I'm here. It's important to you."

"Well, Jesus, you look skinny today. Your shoulder blades almost sliced me when I picked you up, homes!"

"Thanks," I beamed.

Two very young-looking boys approached and greeted Nick. Nick grabbed one of them on the butt and they all started laughing.

"Tony, this is Kevin and Ben."

"Nice to meet you." We all shook hands. "I'm assuming you guys are Lucas's friends?"

"No," said Kevin. "We're friends of Nick's."

"Oh?" I said. "How?"

"Um..." Kevin smiled and looked at Ben.

"We met the other night at Bones," Nick said.

"Ah. Well, that's nice."

"I need another beer. You guys want anything?" Nick asked.

"No we're good," Ben said. Nick made his way toward the bar.

Kevin whispered something into Ben's ear. They were probably talking about me.

"So, how do you know Nick?" Ben asked me.

"We're friends. Well, not like friends like you guys are friends with him." They laughed. "We went to school together."

"Cool," Kevin said. "Do you work in construction too?'

"No. I'm at a desk job," I said.

"What kind of work do you do?"

"Marketing."

"Oh, are you Nick's friend who also works at the arts centre? Nick told me he had a friend who was working two jobs," said Kevin.

"No. He was probably talking about one of our other friends," I quipped.

I wanted to change the subject immediately, but they were too fast with their questions.

"Are you an executive? Do you have your own office?" Kevin asked.

I didn't know how to respond to that. "Um, I have my own cubicle," I said.

Both their eyes lit up.

"That's so cool. You must be an A-Gay!" Kevin said with a big smile.

"A-Gay? Me?" I asked.

"You know, one of those successful, top-level gays," Ben said.

I chuckled. "Far from it."

"Do you own your own place?" Ben asked.

"No, well sort of."

"You have your own space... Oh honey, you're totally an A-Gay! Snaps to that!" Ben and Kevin clinked their glasses.

I laughed. "Thanks. You boys are sweet. How about you? Are you both working or still in school?"

"No, not working," Ben said. "We're both first year U of T."

Oh my God. These boys were eighteen or nineteen. "What are you studying?" I asked.

"I'm taking English and sosc," Ben said.

"Sorry, what's sosc?"

"Sociology," Ben replied. "I'm pre-law."

"Cool," I said. I turned to Kevin. "How about you?"

"I'm pre-med. Taking kin and bio."

"Kin as in kinesiology?"

"Yeah." Kevin nodded.

"Wow. That's great," I said.

"Yeah, we're pretty impressive," Ben said.

"And humble too," I said. They laughed.

"No but for real," Ben continued, "I said to myself, 'self, what do you want to do that will help others and make a shitload of dough,' and I was like helluurrr? I'll be a doctor! Like duh." He took another drink.

"What kind of doctor do you want to be?" I asked.

"I don't know. A rich one?" Ben said. "I love kids so ... maybe a podiatrist?"

Kevin quickly jumped in. "We're totally going to be A-Gays too!"

"Snaps to that too!" Ben said. They laughed and clinked their drinks.

"So what's next for you, Tony?" Kevin asked.

"Next?" I asked.

"Yeah, what do you have planned next? What's the next great thing?"

I laughed. "I'm just trying to make it to the next day."

They laughed. Their naivety and optimism were endearing.

Kevin looked down at his phone. "Oh, Grindr message... hot daddy, eleven o'clock! He said he's near the bathroom. Girl, come with me," he said, pulling Ben away.

Nick returned and handed me a pink drink with a cherry on the side of the glass.

"What is this?" I asked him.

"You'll like it—it's really sweet. It tastes like peaches."

"Thanks. Where's the birthday boy?"

"I don't know," Nick said. "Probably in the back sucking some toddler. Ha!"

Lisa came over and hugged me. "Oh my God, Tony, you made it! And you haven't dashed off yet. I'm so proud of you."

"Thank you," I said.

"You having fun?"

"Actually it's been pretty good. I met a couple of Nick's little friends—they're so cute."

"Great. Let's dance!" Lisa lead me into the sea of twirling gays on the dance floor.

I liked dancing when I first came out. But now I was worried about looking like a stiff old fogey.

Lisa leaned in: "Just enjoy yourself. Let go. Who cares what you look like."

"Right," I said. I closed my eyes and tilted my head back. *Just let go.* I opened my eyes and saw my reflection in a massive disco ball spinning from the ceiling. I looked at my face—I could see my cheekbones even in those tiny swirling mirrors. I was relieved. I started rotating my hips to the music.

"Yas!" yelled Lisa. "That's it, baby girl!" We laughed.

Nick, Lucas, Kevin and Ben joined us. Lucas was so drunk that he lost balance and bumped into another guy; I went over and apologized for him. I was enjoying myself, even letting the boys take group pics of us for Instagram. After an hour or so, my shirt was soaked in sweat. This night was a success—I was having fun and burning calories at the same time.

Lucas turned to Kevin. "Anybody know if Antonio was coming?"

"Who's Antonio? Lisa asked.

"Just one of our other friends. I saw him earlier," Kevin said. He looked around then pointed up. "There he is."

We all looked to where Kevin pointed. There was a tall Latino-looking boy dancing on the side stage. He looked young as well, probably the same age as Kevin and Ben.

His hair fell slightly below his ears in loosely tossed curls that flowed and bounced with the beat of the music. His skin was toasted gold and although he was slim and lanky, I could see his toned physique beneath his white V-neck t-shirt and skinny ripped jeans. His movements were fluid and light, as if he were floating and dancing simultaneously. I wasn't sure if that made sense—my head felt a bit hazy. There were other people dancing around him, but it seemed like he had a huge empty space around him that nobody wanted to invade. He continued spinning around, gracefully moving his arms and twirling his hips. I continued to watch and found that I was staring with my head tilted sideways. I squinted and thought he might be biting his bottom lip. He moved the hair out of his face and looked around until he caught me gazing at him. I thought of the young boys I'd read about in classical civilization books, the ones in Ancient Greece who would wear crowns of leaves on their heads and walk around barefoot and speak in proverbs. His eyes caught the light; they were light brown... hazel, or grey maybe? I don't know if they were twinkling or if it was the reflections of the disco ball. I knew that I should probably look away, but I wasn't able to. Oddly, I thought I saw him wink at me and smile. I looked behind me to see if he was looking at someone else, but nobody was there. He pointed at me and flashed another smile. I looked at him and pointed to myself with a look of puzzlement. He nodded.

He was the most beautiful thing I had ever seen.

Why did he look familiar?

Suddenly the music seemed to slow down, and my vision got blurry. The people around me looked wobbly and strange, and then all went dark. There was a huge crashing thud and a tremendous pain in the back of my head.

Apparently I was out for a good two or three minutes before Lisa poured ice water on my face and woke me up. Drinking alcohol and eating nothing beforehand had been a bad idea. My memories of the night were foggy. For all I knew, that beautiful boy could have been an image in my cloudy head. Like the Virgin Mary or Jesus that my mom always envisioned when we prayed the rosary for all those years.

Chapter 11: Conference Call

"Tony-Tone!" Jell-O was standing behind me.

It was hump day, and I was tired. And I had to teach at Gold's later that day.

"Hi, Victor."

"I just wanted to run through the revisions to our next EFT presentation. Have you got it done yet?"

"No, I haven't." I hadn't been able to get myself to focus on finishing it. Concentration was difficult when the only thing on my mind was food.

"Okay," Jell-O said. "Are you planning to complete it?"

"Yeah. Sorry about that."

Jell-O leaned a little lower, closer to my ear. "You okay?" he asked.

"Yeah. Why?"

"You know you missed our conference call this morning. With that new client. I tried to delay until you joined, but you never did. So we had to go on without you. I had Lauren step in."

Suddenly I remembered. *Shit.*

"Oh my God. Jell—Victor. ... I'm so sorry. I had some stomach issues this morning and got in late."

"That's okay Tony. Just give me a heads-up next time."

"I will for sure. I'll get up to speed with Lauren. Sorry again."

I saw his gaze travel up and down my body. "Okay."

He turned around and walked away, only to turn around and come right back to my cubicle.

"Hey Tony-Tone?" he asked.

"Yes?"

"Did you work late last night?"

"Yeah why?"

"Ernesto told me he found one of the toilets were clogged in the men's bathroom this morning. Apparently, it was covered in puke everywhere. Gross. He asked the cleaning lady who said that she didn't leave it like that when she clocked out. You see anything or anyone last night?"

I'd become a master at holding a straight face. Two nights ago I'd had a big binge with the added treat of a couple of martinis that I enjoyed alone. Even after throwing up as much as I could, I'd still woken up with a hangover, and I was still suffering as I worked into the evening at my cubicle. I'd tried to get rid of it by eating a greasy slice of pizza left over from a catered meeting, but that had turned into a binge and I'd ended up eating more than half of the box. I still had work to finish, so I'd had no choice but to get it out of my system at the office. But the toilet wasn't flushing properly. I never thought vomit could clog a toilet. I'd pushed on the lever repeatedly with no success. So I just left, hoping the janitor would clean up the mess I had created, and in the morning, all would have been forgotten.

Apparently not.

"Huh. Weird. No, I didn't see anything," I said.

"Okay, thanks." Jell-O turned around and walked away.

Chapter 12: I Know Your Name

Saturday morning at Gold's Community Arts Centre; I was nodding off at my desk, having finished a report for Jell-O pretty late the night before.

Rita, the centre administrator, handed me my class list for the summer term, starting the following Saturday. Registration was on a first come, first serve basis. The first twenty students got in, then we put the next five on the waiting list. I had to make the calls informing parents that their child couldn't get into the course.

"Hi there, Mrs. Lombardi. I'm calling to let you know that although we put Matthew on the waitlist for Intro to Acrylic Painting, nobody has dropped out. So, I'm sorry, but we're over capacity. Maybe next term?" I always try to sound as robotic as possible. It used to be hard to keep rejecting the children, but I got used to it.

"Okay, thank you for letting me know," Mrs. Lombardi said.

But not every parent was so understanding. Some expressed their displeasure through some choice phrases that I got accustomed to hearing: "Let me talk to your supervisor!" or, "That's impossible! I registered yesterday 10 minutes before the deadline!" or, "But my son is a way better artist than the other kids!"

I found that apologizing repeatedly was the best way to get through the calls, rather than say what I wanted to say: "Your kid can't be that talented. And even if he was, he's not going to make it as an artist. This ain't the movies. He's not the special snowflake you think he is, ma'am."

The instructors were setting up their classrooms. I pasted on my smile, waved my courtesy hellos and recited my pleasantries to the familiar faces: "I'm good. Busy busy. How about yourself?"

Some of the new ones were in the hallway outside my classroom. They were young and upbeat, chatting in a circle, all clutching their Starbucks cups. But there was one guy who seemed to be the centre of the conversation. The others circled him, careful not to invade the empty space around him. He glanced at me a couple of times. As the group dispersed, he picked up his box of supplies and began walking toward me. His movements were light and smooth, as if he was floating. His loose curls bounced up and down with each step. He flashed a smile and stopped in front of me.

He looked like that boy in the club the night of the party. *Antonio, was it?*

He seemed to recognize me too.

It was the same guy, standing before me.

"Hello," he said.

"Hi," I replied.

"I'm one of the new instructors. Antonio. Painting with Oils."

"Nice to meet you."

Pause.

"We've already met," he said, still smiling.

"I'm sorry?"

"I know you. Or I mean, I saw you... last week at that club?"

I tried to act casual. "Oh, maybe?"

"Yeah, you're Nick's friend? You met a couple of my girls, Ben and Kevin? I heard you passed out that night. You okay?"

"Oh, right. Yeah, that's me. I usually turn into a pumpkin after ten-thirty. I'm fine now, thanks."

He extended his hand. "Nice to meet you."

I shook it.

"I'm—"

He cut me off. "Oh, I know your name."

"You do?" I asked.

"Yeah." The sides of his lips curled.

"Really? What's my name?" I smiled too.

His face went serious. "You're sexy."

Was that a joke? "Uh… "

His smile returned. "I'm joking, I'm joking. Well, not really."

I relaxed. "You're funny. I'm Tony."

"Hi Tony. Charmed I'm sure. I'm Antonio." He reached out to shake my hand again. "We're twinzies."

"What?"

"We have the same name. We're pretty much the same person."

"Oh yeah," I chuckled. *You're just the taller and beautiful version of me.*

Pause.

"What classroom are you in?" I asked.

"310F."

"I'll call Rita to book the elevator so you can move in your supplies."

"Thanks."

He gave me one more smile, and then twirled around and floated away. I looked down at my shirt. There were sweat stains under my arms, unusual because I was always cold.

I had finally finished the revised presentation for EFT, two days after a follow-up meeting was supposed to take place. I had asked to reschedule to Tuesday because I couldn't get myself to focus and finish the presentation. I said that we were having some software issues and had to do further testing. They believed me.

I was supposed to lead the meeting, but I wasn't feeling well. Jell-O and Lauren-the-intern took over while I tried to take minutes. Matt and Sunny noticed me shifting back and forth in my chair. Sweat streamed down behind my ears and I had to keep wiping my forehead.

"You okay, Tony?" Matt asked.

"I'm fine. Continue."

The night before, I'd been in a panic getting prepared for this meeting. I couldn't get my numbers to work and Excel kept crashing on me. Finally, I gave up and printed the final copies without the budget, hoping nobody would notice. On the way home, I stopped by this little burrito joint about five minutes from my house. I needed to calm down.

"I'll have two large steak burritos, extra cheese," I said to the cashier. "And two fully loaded nachos and two churros." Easily 2,800 calories.

After a few minutes she handed me three paper bags, shiny with grease stains. "One of the burritos might have less guacamole. We ran out," she said.

"That's okay, I'll give my friend that one." We both laughed.

I stopped by the grocery store to pick up some ice cream. Dessert—whatever it was; cake, cookies, pie—was not complete without ice cream. Coincidentally, Häagen-Dazs was on sale, so I bought four pints. *On sale—it would be stupid not to buy extra.*

It usually didn't take much time for me to finish my food, whether I was eating with friends or bingeing alone at home. I polished off the burritos and nachos within twenty minutes. I knew I should take more time to actually savour my food, but because I was always starving, my senses tended to get overwhelmed with the flavour and I'd end up inhaling everything. Wrappers were scattered all over my kitchen table and floor, as if some thief had broken into the house to snatch food and run.

I warmed the churros and shoveled out about half a pint of ice cream on top of them. *I worked hard. I finished the stupid presentation. I deserve this. And plus, I'm just going to get rid of it all anyway.* I salivated with each swallow.

But thirty minutes later, when I stuck my fingers down my throat, nothing would come up. I tried again and again, shoving at different speeds, then the other hand, then my toothbrush. Nothing worked.

I have to get this out, I thought. *I cannot keep all this food.* My mind was racing. *Fuck, I gotta get this out or I'll be a balloon!*

An hour later, my eyes puffy and tearing, the veins on my neck and forehead bulging, my shirt soaked in sweat, I had nothing to show for it except a few splatters of blood. But I was determined. I could *not* keep it all in.

I pulled out my supply of laxatives and diuretics. I took four of each (a hundred milligrams and twenty-five milligrams, respectively), along with my other pills, and then went to bed. Though they were less effective in getting all the food out, laxatives and diuretics were always my last resort if vomiting didn't work.

I woke up in the morning with stabbing pains in my stomach. I went to the bathroom twice before I left the house, and another two times at the office before the meeting with EFT. I couldn't believe how much was coming out of me. By the last time, I was excreting only liquid. I thought I had rid myself of all of it.

But as the meeting started, my stomach continued to turn and rumble; I shifted back and forth and sweated like a drug addict in withdrawal. Something hot ran through me, intense pressure building in my gut. I clenched as tight as I could. My belly pushed against my belt.

I could no longer hold it. I stood up. They all looked at me.

"Excuse me. I'll be right back," I said, and I rushed out of the room.

As soon as I sat down, everything inside me exploded into the bowl. Water splashed back at my ass. It burned between my cheeks. When I wiped, the toilet paper came away bright pink with blood. I must have ripped something.

I cleaned myself up as fast as I could and hurried back to the meeting room.

"Tony, you're back. Great," Jell-O said. "I was just about to start going through the logistics. Or did you want to?"

"No, I think you got this, Victor," I said. I tried to sit farther away from everyone for fear they might notice a smell.

A few minutes later the pains returned. *This can't be happening.* I couldn't run out of the room for a second time. My insides grumbled softly at first, then went into full thunder mode. Everybody tried to ignore the noises, although I saw Matt and Sunny exchange raised eyebrows. Sweat gathered on my forehead, highlighting my embarrassment.

I stood up again and walked toward the door. I didn't even look at their faces as I left the room. "I'm so sorry guys, I'm just not feeling well." I could feel their eyes on my back.

The next day, Jell-O called me into a room for a chat.

"PIP is short for Performance Improvement Plan. It outlines a series of actions that you will be required to complete on an ongoing basis to get you back on track. You will check in with me when you come in each morning, when you leave and come back from lunch, and when you leave for the day. We'll have a daily meeting at 9:15 a.m., where a representative from HR and I will review your tasks for the day. We'll also audit your work from the day before to ensure it was completed. If you fail to finish what was assigned to you, you will need to provide an incident form detailing the cause of the delay. You'll also use the form to document any errors that you have made on work. I'll email the template to you. Lastly, you'll keep a log in Excel of all the activities you work on every hour, which I'll also send you. The log will be handy as a reference in cases where you have to fill out an incident form.

"I'm having Lauren take over your work on the Bellows account, the EFT project and invoicing. A lot of your work for the next little while will be items she delegates to you.

"If you reach three incident forms, in combination with continued difficulties arriving on time, calling in sick, or extended washroom breaks, we will have to take disciplinary measures, which could potentially involve your dismissal. Do you understand what I'm saying, Tony?"

Jell-O's monologue lost me. As he kept talking, I stared at his belly.

"Tony?" he said, "what are you staring at?"

I raised my eyes from his midsection to his face. "Yes. Sorry Victor. Yes, I get it."

"Okay, sign here." Jell-O handed me the papers and pointed to the signature line. Then he leaned back in his chair. "Tony, is there anything you want to talk about?"

His voice sounded different than usual. It didn't have the usual upbeat, business-savvy, radio-announcer sound to it. It was lower and slower. Genuine.

"No. I'm okay."

He sighed. "Tone, I've worked with you for how many years now? I don't want to have to see you like this, big guy."

"It's fine. I'll be fine."

"My door is open anytime if you need help or anything."

"Thank you, Victor. That's nice."

"Did you want to go home early?"

"No."

"Okay. How about you just walk Lauren through the EFT account and anything else you want, and then head out."

"Sure."

He left the meeting room. It was the least dramatic exit I had ever seen him make.

Chapter 14: Kaleidoscope

The next evening I went to Gold's, not to teach a class, but because Jackie, the pottery instructor, had emailed me to come to her classroom. She wanted to order more tables to display the students' work. Since I'd been an instructor there for seven years, the staff relied more on me for information than on poor Rita, who always had more to do than she had time for.

"To be honest, I don't know if we'll get approval for it. I know there's not much room in the program budget right now," I said. "Can't you put their items on the floor?"

"No, I don't think that'll work. We're dealing with clay and stone and porcelain," Jackie said. "The students will think we don't give a shit about their work."

"Well, we don—" I stopped myself and looked around. The tables she did have were cluttered with so many pieces that even the slightest bump could cause a number of pieces to topple over and break. But I knew the centre didn't have the money for anything, even tables. Every year the arts funding from the government decreased. "I don't know. It might come down to taking some tables from another classroom, or using private funding," I said.

"Private funding? I spend way too much of my own money on teaching already," she said.

"I know," I said. "I'll have Rita check prices and get back to you."

As I left Jackie's room, I saw room 310F across the hall. Painting with Oil.

Antonio's classroom.

The door was slightly open; through the crevice I could see a vibrant burst of colour. I walked over and looked in—the classroom was empty.

The walls were hung with canvases. The subjects of the paintings varied—fruit, figures, faces, sunsets, cars. Others were abstract, with shapes and patterns random and indecipherable. Most looked finished, a few halfway done. A small number of them were bare, with only a streak, or a dot, or a blob of colour. None of the canvases were square with the wall or even with each other—it was as if they'd been tossed up on the walls like darts. There were about fifteen easels in the centre of the room, each holding a painting of a male mannequin. Although it was in the same pose on all the canvases, the mannequin looked different in every one. Tacked to a bulletin board were newspaper clippings, pages of poems ripped out of books, colourful photographs, and flyers about other workshops, art galleries and art shows. Clay sculptures and even papier maché balloons crowded desks in the corners of the room.

Some of the canvases were still wet. The smell of the paint was so strong it made me woozy. I kept looking around in circles—there was so many colours and shapes and patterns to take in that I didn't know where to focus. Sensory overload.

I had stepped into a chaotic, exhilarating kaleidoscope.

A large portrait of a woman's face called to me. I'm not an art connoisseur, but this painting was flawless and lifelike. Her large round eyes, hazel or light brown—greyish maybe, like Antonio's— seemed to project outward from the wall. She had long, wavy brown hair that ended at her shoulders, blending into the fabric of her dark clothing. Like a modern take on Mona Lisa. Her eyes followed me. I was fixated.

"That's my mother."

I turned around. Antonio stood in the doorway.

"Do you like it?" he asked.

"She's beautiful."

"Yeah, and she knows it. Oh Dios mio." He smirked.

"Did you paint this?" I asked.

"Yeah. Took about four months."

"She must love it."

"She hasn't seen it. If she did, she'd hang it at our front entrance." He chuckled.

I laughed.

"I think I might give it to her for her birthday or something," he said. "It's a bit weird having her big face watching me here every day."

"You look like her."

Beside the portrait hung a handful of other paintings that stood out, one of a grizzly bear with a cub, another of flowers.

"Did you paint these too?" I asked.

"Yes, actually."

"What's this one called?" I pointed.

"To Trap a Bear."

"And this one?"

"The Wings of the Roses."

"Amazing," I said.

"The title of it is from a line in one of my favourite poems."

"Courage, by Anne Sexton."

"You know it?"

It was one of my favourite poems too. I knew it well. I wanted to impress him, but I hesitated; I didn't want to come off as pretentious. Finally I put caution aside and recited a snippet: "you powdered your sorrow / you gave it a back rub / and then you covered it with a blanket / and after it had slept a while / it woke to the wings of the roses / and was transformed."

He stared at me, his mouth half smiling, half open in shock. So sweet. "I love how you have that memorized."

"I'm a bit of a poem nerd, but I love that one," I said. "Another good one with flowers is 'Tulips' by Sylvia Plath. It's amazing."

"I'll have to check it out."

I continued studying the paintings. "Do you paint these by looking, or does this come from your head?"

"Both. However I feel, I guess. Sometimes I just let my hands go and see what shows up on the canvas."

"I'll have to take a class with you sometime."

"Well I'd love to teach you, Tony."

Does he talk like that to everyone?

I headed toward the door. But the flowers—the "wings of the roses"—caught my eye and I stopped to look again. They made me think of my mother's garden. "These roses really are beautiful," I said. "Can I ask you something?"

"Yes?"

"I don't know if you're free maybe tomorrow night, if you'd like to go for a drink?" My voice cracked. I cleared my throat. "Or maybe just a coffee sometime, whenever?"

"I'm not free tomorrow," he said.

"Okay. Maybe on the weekend?"

"I'm not free on the weekend either."

"Oh." I looked at the floor. "Okay. I get it." *What was I thinking?*

"I'm free tonight though."

I looked up. He was smiling.

"You are?" I asked.

"Yeah."

I was supposed to have an appointment with Dr. Tee. He had squeezed me into a later time to accommodate me. I decided that I wouldn't go, and smiled at Antonio. "Okay."

Chapter 15: Memories Erased and Replaced

"Where do you want to go?" I asked as we got into my car, a beat up 2008 Toyota Corolla that I got for $2,000 and my Mom's 1997 Chevy Cavalier as a trade in.

"I'm good with whatever," Antonio said.

"Anywhere you want."

I turned the car on and connected my phone. An audio self-help book blared out from the speakers—*The Mindful Way through Depression.* I fumbled with the phone to turn it off.

"What are you listening to?" Antonio asked.

I quickly switched to the radio. "Nothing. Just some new age stuff, you know?"

It was Thursday night. I got paid last Friday from Melo but almost all of it went toward the mortgage. My car insurance payment came out on Monday. I bought some laundry detergent and toilet paper at Walmart on Tuesday. I was getting paid from Gold's at midnight. So how much did I have in my chequing account? Maybe ninety bucks, or eighty-five? Shit, did my phone bill come out already? Maybe I could use my credit card for dinner, but I was pretty sure I was close to maxed out and couldn't remember if I'd paid the last minimum.

Why couldn't he be free tomorrow night? At least I'd have my next pay cheque and could take him to a nice dinner.

As my thoughts on my sorry broke ass rambled on, I realized this was the closest I had ever been to Antonio physically. I couldn't help but notice that he actually smelled sweet. Like dessert. Cake.

"Anywhere?" he asked.

"Yeah."

I was worried. We were near Yorkville. The expensive places I used to go to with Ken, after which I'd post photos of the plates on my social media.

"You know what?" Antonio said.

"What?"

"I feel like pancakes!"

I had to laugh. I could afford pancakes. All right, sure. There's Fran's on College."

Antonio opened the door to the restaurant for me. The hostess was probably in her late 50s.

"Hi," she said to me, in a tired voice.

Antonio walked in after me, and her face lit up as she greeted him: "Well, hello there."

"Hello," Antonio said. "How are you?"

"Very well. Thank you for asking. You need a table?"

"Yes, for two please."

"Right this way."

She led us to a dimly lit booth in the corner.

"Do you know her?" I asked him.

"No."

Our waitress arrived.

"Hey there… Elizabeth," he said, eyeing her nametag. She practically blushed. Yet another middle-aged woman who seemed to have eyes for Antonio. I couldn't blame her.

Antonio ordered the Grand Double Breakfast: two eggs, two pieces of toast, two strips of bacon, two sausages and two pancakes. It was 1,300 calories.

"I'll have a small garden salad, dressing on the side. And a Diet Coke," I told Elizabeth.

"I'm sorry?" Antonio said. "You're having a salad? Honey, please."

"Yeah, it's fine. I like salad," I said.

"No, you don't."

"Yes, I do."

"Nope," Antonio said. He turned the waitress. "Lizzy darling, he'll have the same thing as me." He looked back at me with a smile.

"Sure thing," she said. She looked at me. "How could you say no to that smile?"

"I guess I can't."

Shit. 1,300 calories. I'd have to double my fat burners and take an extra half tablet of laxatives after I threw this up. 1,300 calories. I'd also do an extra half-hour of cardio tomorrow.

I fiddled with a napkin. "So, how are you liking it at the centre so far?"

"Oh, I love it! The students have been great and everybody has been awesome."

"Do you teach oil painting only? It looks like you could teach sketching or sculpture too?"

"I could. I kind of just go from one medium to another, depending on how I feel. Whenever I feel like I want to really get in there, you know, get my hands dirty, I'll work on sculpture. Then a few days later I'll feel like working on a flat surface, so I paint. Depends on the day. Anyway, I don't want to bore you with that stuff."

"No, it's all good. I'm interested. At one point I pursued the arts too."

"Oh yeah?"

"Yeah. I took a writing course at Gold's when I was young."

"And... ?"

1,300 calories.

"And what? Oh, I wasn't very good at it. So I stopped.

"But did you enjoy it? That's the important thing."

"I did."

Elizabeth came with the orders. "The plates are hot, so be careful."

The plates were also huge. The first one had the eggs, meat and toast on it; there was a separate plate for the pancakes.

I was anxious. I needed to make a plan. Maybe I could eat as little as possible, and then take the rest home and throw it out. Or eat as slowly as I could, wait till the end to finish the food, drop Antonio off quickly, and then get to my toilet as soon as possible—maybe I'd make it within the one-hour window.

Quantify. Cut cut cut.

"Yas Queen!" Antonio exclaimed with joy, beaming at the waitress. "Lizzy honey, you are my hero!"'

She laughed. "Oh, I just love you. You're adorable. Let me know if you need anything, okay?"

"Oh Dios mio! Well, hellllurrr there, pancakes!" Antonio said goofily, pushing the eggs aside. I laughed. It was like watching a kid at Christmas.

"Oh wait!" he said. "I need to get this on the 'gram!" He took out his phone and snapped a picture.

He took a knife and spread butter across the pancakes. Then he ripped open four sugar packets and sprinkled them overtop. Finally, he picked up the bottle of maple syrup and drowned the pancakes until the syrup dripped off the plate. He took a bite, threw his head back and moaned.

"Oh em gee! Morgasmic!" he said. "You ever had a mouth orgasm?"

I watched in awe. Antonio was over the top, and I loved it, every bit of it. All that flamboyance on full display, like a peacock proudly showing his feathers. As if his response to a "masculine man" on Grindr would be autogenerated: "fuck you, you're just stupid."

"Oh my God, don't judge me, okay honey?" he said.

"So you like your syrup with pancakes, eh?" I smirked.

"Ha-ha."

"I'm kidding, I'm kidding."

"I like my stuff sweet, okay? I don't do anything half-assed. Everything to the extreme!"

"That's cool. I'm not judging."

Antonio stuck his fork into another piece. Syrup dripped from the fork. He held it near my face.

"Want some?" he asked.

"No, I have my own, I'm good."

"No, just taste it with the butter and sugar, it's so good!"

"No, it's okay."

"Just open your mouth and shove it in!" he said sternly, then breaking into a smile. "Don't make me have a hissy fit, Toners!"

I giggled. "Okay."

"But you have to close your eyes. It makes it more exciting."

"Sure."

I closed my eyes and opened my mouth. I felt the sweet squishy pancake on my tongue. Like eating a pillow soaked in sugary syrup. My saliva glands raced.

It was amazing. "Mmm. Morgasm."

"Isn't that heaven?" he said. "And with the syrup crystallizing the sugar, you get some crunch! Hallelujah!"

"That is pretty game-changing."

"Do I know how to pimp out my hotcakes or what?"

I ate as slow as I could; each bite raised my anxiety level. I felt my face expand as I swallowed. I had never eaten this much without being 100% sure I could purge it soon after.

"Honey, why aren't you eating? I've inhaled this plate," Antonio said.

I was amazed. His plate was clean. How did he do that? How did he do that without restraint or worry?

How could he just eat it and enjoy it and have that be the end of it?

"I'm just taking my time. I usually don't go for huge meals like this," I said.

"Well oink oink, thanks for calling me a pig, Tony."

"No, I didn't mean it like that."

"I'm kidding. I'm sorry if I forced that on you. I just wanted to celebrate, you know."

"Celebrate what?"

"Nothing really. Well, everything. That it's a nice night, that we're here, you know what I mean."

I smiled and nodded.

"So, we were talking about writing…" he said. "What happened after you took the course at Gold's?"

"Well, I wanted to keep going—I dreamed of doing something with art, a writer, or maybe a filmmaker. But my mother wouldn't have any of it. It was either medicine, law, or business for me. She'd say, 'What am I going to tell everyone? That you want to make a living expressing yourself? I didn't work two jobs so you could go gallivanting around doodling with paint and all this nonsense!' I was like, 'no, Mom, I'd write too,' and she was like, 'Write what? A poem about how poor you're gonna be?' She was such a smartass."

He laughed. "So what did you do?"

"I did what everyone else did who hated all subjects except for English and art… I went to business school at U of T, and flunked my way out with flying colours. I ended up taking some writing classes at Humber. And now I teach it to kids, so I guess that's something."

Antonio laughed. "I've heard that Asian parents would rather die than not see their kids do something huge."

"That's true."

"How's your mom feel about you now?"

"She's dead."

Antonio's face turned serious.

"So I guess it worked out for her," I chuckled.

"Oh shit, sorry … but… that's a sick joke," he said, leaning back in his seat.

"I know. I'm going to hell. Sorry." I fiddled with my utensils. "Can we talk about you now?"

"Sure."

"You must love being an artist. It must feel great to make such beautiful things."

"Yeah, I guess. But for me it's all about the process."

"You're going to pursue it right?"

"Yeah, I don't have choice… I love it. It's a bit out there, but I want to get into NAFA in Montreal."

"NAFA?"

"The National Academy of Fine Arts? It's the most renowned arts school in Canada. And I hear they're pretty good about supporting students in doing their own stuff rather than forcing them to follow a program."

"Good for you. And then what would you want to do after that? Be a prof?" I asked.

"I don't know. Haven't thought about it. I'll figure it out as I go."

I wanted to know everything about him. He said he lived with his mother and his little sister. He never mentioned his father. He had a second job to help his mother with the bills.

"I work at the Flamingo bar part-time. We should go sometime," he said.

He looked at my plate. "Are you gonna eat that sausage?"

"No, go for it. Take whatever," I said.

He reached over and helped himself. "Thanks."

I took another sip of my Diet Coke. Had to make sure I got that carbonated beverage in for later.

"So what do you like to do?" he asked.

"Well, aside from working part-time at Gold's, I work for a consulting company Monday to Friday."

"Oh. Is that what you *like* to do?"

"Oh sorry. What do I like to do? Reading, classical music, theatre, I guess? Wow, I sound like a pretentious douche."

"Not at all."

Antonio looked down at my plate again.

"You know what, Antonio, just finish the plate or have it packed and take it home."

"You sure?"

"Yeah. I'm stuffed."

"You barely ate anything."

Elizabeth brought over the bill. It was $56.50. I was sure I had that in my account. Even if I didn't, there was always overdraft.

"How much do I owe you?" Antonio asked.

"No worries," I said. "I got it."

"You sure?"

"Yes."

"Well in that case, Lizzy, can I get a lobster?"

Elizabeth hollered. She ate up every one of his jokes.

After I paid, Antonio looked at me with those big round greyish-brown-or-were-they-hazel eyes. He was smiling. I was getting self-conscious and looked at the window, trying to find my reflection. *Do I look okay? Do I look thin?*

I looked back at him. "Antonio?"

"Yup."

"Can I ask you something?"

"Yeah."

"How old are you?"

"Twenty-one."

Twenty-one. Holy shit. I've judged Nick for this, now I'm the same. I'm that perv.

"Oh."

He fiddled with his hair a bit, and tucked it behind his ear.

"Aren't you going to ask me how old I am?" I asked.

"No. Does it matter?"

"I guess not," I said. *Phew.*

As we left the restaurant, I noticed a bunch of teenage boys smoking on the other side of the parking lot. We heard them laughing as we walked toward the car.

"Hey, homoville is that way, faggots!" one called as we got in.

Antonio looked at him and shouted "Yeah, but your mom is this way, asshole!" before slamming the door.

All the boys turned around, shocked. Through the windshield, I could see one of them mouth "Da fuck?!"

"Shit, Tony, let's go!"

I sped out as fast as I could as they swore at us. I don't remember the last time I laughed so hard.

Antonio lived in Parkdale. The roads were full of potholes, making my car jump. There was garbage on the sidewalks.

"Right here," he said.

We stopped at a dark brown apartment on King Street. Air-conditioners filled most of the windows. A couple of men sat smoking and chatting in front of the building.

It was 11:00 p.m. "Hopefully my mom and my sister aren't waiting for me." Antonio said.

"Thank you. That was really nice."

"No, thank you for dinner. I promise I'll put out next time."

"Ha-ha."

He reached over and turned the radio down, staring at me with those eyes.

"Goodnight," he said.

"Goodn—""

Before I could finish the word, he leaned in and gave me a peck on the cheek. I could smell cake coming off his skin again. He grabbed the take-out bag, got out of the car and flew toward the entrance.

"Howdy guys!" he said to the men at the doorway. They nodded back.

He turned around and smiled at me. He did a little dance—some sort of shimmy—waved, and then turned around and disappeared.

I drove home quickly and ran to the toilet. When I was done, I cleaned up, took my pills—including a double dose of fat burners and laxatives—iced my cheeks for fifteen minutes, and then lay down in bed.

I turned on Rachmaninoff's Piano Concerto no. 2, and replayed everything that happened in my mind. For so long, I had associated negative memories with that music. Finally, I had found something worthy to replace them with.

The concerto would be the soundtrack for a new montage of images in my head: daydreaming about Antonio at my cubicle, romantic dinners with him, Lisa and Nick making fun of me for "babysitting," kissing him in the car before dropping him off at home, and then going home and *not* purging what I had just consumed. How nice would that feel? Maybe it didn't have to be Antonio; just the thought of being close to somebody, loving somebody, made me both excited and terrified. I barely slept that night.

The next morning I went to Melo and sleep-walked through the workday, only perking up in the evening, when I was able to get a last-minute appointment with Dr. Tee.

"You were supposed to be here yesterday, Tony," Dr. Tee said.

I nodded. "Sorry."

"Why are you here?" he asked.

I cleared my throat. "I want to tell you something."

"Yes?"

The look on Antonio's face when the pancakes arrived at the table the night before flashed into my mind.

"Dr. Tee... I need help."

Part Two

Chapter 16: Rosaries

Memory is my enemy. It never fails me, although I often wish it did.

I remember the look on my mother's face when the oncologist told us she had reached the palliative stage. He gave her the option of remaining in the palliative care unit at the hospital, or staying home and being cared for by me with the help of visiting nurses. Her eyes widened in fear and confusion; she suddenly became a lost little girl. Ultimately, chose to be remain at home, thinking she'd be more "comfortable."

I had been promoted from closeted 18-year-old to palliative care nurse.

I'd never realized how much of a spoiled child I was until I won that job. I didn't know how to cook. I had no idea how to pay bills. It scared me to think I'd have to maintain the house, and what it represented—a life that was built by her, for me.

One of the duties of caregiver included cleaning and re-bandaging my mother's chest. In the fall of her diagnosis, the little lump that had appeared below her neck metastasized to two areas on her liver. Within three months, the tumour had grown into a tennis-ball-sized lump on her breast bone. Then, inexplicably, a month later, it changed shape and flattened itself across her chest and part of her breasts.

The oncologist brushed over the explanation: "Tumours change shape. It happens."

It was a shield, protecting her from health, from a cure. I put my finger to it—it was hard as bone. Is that what death felt like? She often looked down at it, and I'd try to divert her attention to her rosary, or her prayers, or church. Anything.

Then it changed again. Mom's flat chest rose up like a volcano, bigger than before. By spring, it was poking through her shirt enough to draw stares as I pushed her wheelchair through the grocery store. This time, the tumour did not flatten. It got so big that the skin her on her chest began to crack. Days went by, and the volcano erupted.

It happens.

The top of the tumour revealed itself to be rock-like, and covered in bumps and crevices. Blood and some kind of pus-like fluid oozed slowly from the peak and pooled over my mother's body. If she shifted in her bed, the fluid spilled over onto the bedsheets or upward to her neck. I was constantly wiping her down; I could not let the lava get near her face.

The blood kept soaking through the bandage and hardening on her torn skin. She was constantly complaining of itchiness—she wanted to scratch it off. Sometimes she'd ask me, only half joking, to get a baseball bat and beat it off like a piñata. It would have felt good to do that—to smash the tumour to smithereens. Or to hold it in my hand and squeeze until my knuckles turned white, suffocating it to death.

Finally I'd had enough. I pulled a visiting nurse, Barb, out into the hallway.

"Forgive my language, but can't we cut that fucking thing out of her chest?" I said. "She looks like a mutant. And it's scaring her. Can't we just cut it out?"

I could tell Barb had known the question was coming, and she'd been dreading to have to answer it.

"It's difficult, Tony. The tumour is attached to her breast bone and parts of her collar bone. Even if they cut off the part that's out, the cancer would still be in the bones. It would just grow again. And the skin is broken in so many places—I don't know how they'd be able to close it."

"This is ridiculous. I want to talk the oncologist."

"Tony, I already have. I've had the same conversation."

"And what'd he say?"

"He said there's no point. That it would do more damage to your mother than good."

"No point?"

"Yes... I'm sorry, Tony."

"No point because she's going to die anyway, right?"

"I'm sorry."

"You all said it was good for her to be cared for at home because she had her choices and her dignity. Look at her." I was furious.

Changing the dressing was like performing surgery. Pull off the old dressing slow enough not to tear her skin. Remove any remaining bandage adhesive or cotton stuck mixed with discharge around and on the tumour with water and saline. Dab and wipe lightly to minimize bleeding. Luckily, my mom was always so drugged with morphine that she couldn't feel any pain. But when she looked down at what I was doing, her eyes would grow panicked and she'd turn back into that little girl.

"Don't look, I told you, Mom," I'd say. "Just keep praying on your rosary." She'd look away and clutch it, reciting her prayers.

God, can you hear us? If you are as great as mom often says, how can you let this be happening?

It's hard to describe the smell of cancer. It's rusty, mouldy... rotted. Slow decay. I'd redress the tumour and watch the white bandage quickly turn red, as if there was no point in changing it in the first place.

It was almost impossible to hold back my tears when I was with her, but I was determined. My mother, who had raised me on her own, was now a patient of her child, who was still a child himself. When I felt my eyes well up, I'd leave the room. I wouldn't let her see me cry.

I couldn't have her think I was less of a man.

Sometimes I'd hide in the basement to bury the sound of my sobbing. I hung the laundry down there to dry. Seeing my mother's clothes pinned up, I realized they would never be worn again. All that would remain of her would be these clothes. Sometimes I'd pick up a shirt she'd worn and smell it; I'd consider not washing it, just so I'd wouldn't lose the scent.

Other times I would drown out my crying in the bathroom with the tap running or the toilet flushing. I'd come back to her room, my face puffy and red, and act as if nothing had happened. I'd try to avoid eye contact, but I knew she knew.

Mom's weight rapidly decreased because she stopped eating, claiming that the chemotherapy had taken away her appetite, and that all food made her nauseous. At first, I tried to cook her small, healthy meals—soup, a piece of fish, a salad maybe—but she ate less and less. Some fruit? No. Then I started bringing her all her favourite guilty pleasures. Anything to get her to eat. I'd drive to KFC, or McDonald's, or Cinnabon, but she still refused. Her five-foot frame went from 125 pounds to seventy in five months. Her bones protruded from her face and torso; her elbows and knees were bigger than her arms and legs. She lost all her muscle, and eventually she was so weak that she couldn't walk.

I got more frustrated the more she disappeared on me. "Mom, just eat it," I pleaded once with a spoonful of rice. "Just eat, please!"

"No," she said. "I don't feel good."

"Just eat, please."

"No."

"Goddam just eat, Mom. Look at you!" I shoved the spoon right to her mouth. She just turned her face away.

"I said no!"

"You're going to eat this now! Do you hear me?"

She smacked the utensil out of my hand, knocking it to the floor. Food scattered across the carpet.

I lost it. "Fuck, if you don't eat you're not going to get better! Do you get that?!"

She started crying. "Stop yelling at me! Please. I feel sick. Just let me sleep!"

I shook my head and stormed out of the room. I could hear her crying from down the hall.

I read somewhere that a piece of your heart breaks every time you hear your mother cry.

We went through this every day. She'd refuse to eat, and I'd yell. She'd cry alone in her bed, her body shrinking into her growing tumour. I cried too, alone, in the bathroom or the basement, tears and hope flowing from my eyes and down the drain. Every day, five days a week, for eight months.

Barb told me that I was making a classic care giver mistake: when the sick person you care for—who often happens to be someone you love very much—doesn't get better, you project your anger and frustration on them.

"You're in pain, Tony, I understand that," Barb said. "But so is she. Don't take it out on her."

"But how is she going to get better if she doesn't eat?" I asked.

"Tony. I've told you this before. She's not going to get better. You need to be realistic here."

I'm grateful that my mother had prayer in her life. It provided a way to cope with it all; she prayed and prayed on that pearl rosary of hers, keeping her hopes alive, right until the day she passed away.

God, I guess you didn't hear us.

I'm not much of a religious person, but eventually, I went and bought myself a rosary. I needed a way to cope too.

Yes, memory was indeed my enemy. But so was belief. The possibility of improvement, the tiny chance at happiness. Hope dangled itself in front of me, taunted me, until I tried to reach it and missed, and my mother drifted away like a speck of dust in the wind.

Once I told Dr. Tee about my eating disorder, the focus of our sessions changed accordingly. Sometimes he'd ask me about the details of each binge and purge—what happened the day leading up to it; how I felt before bingeing (anxious and excited), during (euphoric and electric) and after (panicked); how I felt before vomiting (even more panicked) and after (relieved, ashamed and guilty). He asked about how I viewed my body, pointing out that all my responses included comparing myself to others. I told him about the people I compared myself to: wealthy professionals with gym memberships, spouses, kids and some perfect-looking dog. "Basically, perfect living Ken dolls."

"How do you know they have amazing lives?" Dr. Tee asked.

"Because they tell me. Either in person but mostly through social media."

Dr. Tee shook his head.

"I know," I said, "I'm not supposed to look at that stuff, but I can't help it."

"Is there something specific that you're looking for when you're online?"

"I guess I want some evidence that their lives aren't perfect, so mine will seem less bad. Yes, I'm a bitter Barbie."

Dr. Tee chuckled. Bitter Barbie was one of my catch phrases, I guess.

"I guess I can't accept that things haven't turned out for me the way I wanted, when I've been working my ass off and I think I'm a quote-unquote *good person.*"

Dr. Tee scribbled something on his notepad, then looked at me. "I'm sorry to tell you this, Tony. But life doesn't owe you anything."

BAM. Mic dropped. Dr. Tee always gave it to me hard and straight. It was painful to hear, but I appreciated his honesty.

"I guess you're right," I said begrudgingly.

He introduced some exercises for me to do outside our sessions called Cognitive Behavioural Therapy, or CBT, which, according to the pamphlets was "a problem-focused and goal-oriented form of psychotherapy that helps people examine and change their thought process when dealing with emotional difficulties."

One exercise was to keep a food log. That was nearly impossible at first, because I didn't want to see on paper—let alone think about—what I ate, and how much, and how quickly.

Another exercise was to write down all the times I found myself trying to read the minds of people around me when I felt they were judging me on my appearance. The exercise asked me to think about what those judgments would be ("he's fat," "his face is so round," "he's ugly"), and consider what I would tell a friend who was having those same thoughts.

"I actually liked that exercise," I said.

"And what did you decide you'd tell a friend who might be thinking the same thing?"

"I'd say, 'relax bitch, no one's looking at you.'"

Dr. Tee laughed. "I hope you'd be a little nicer than that."

"Well, yeah. I'd also ask my friend how he could he rationally think he was overweight, when his BMI was 18.4."

"Good. So have you said this to yourself?"

"I have. Sometimes it makes sense. But other times, I just can't make myself believe it."

Dr. Tee wrote on his pad again. "At least you're trying. This is progress."

"Yeah?"

"Definitely."

Dr. Tee pulled some papers from his desk and handed them to me. He cleared his throat. "There's this place called the Light House just north of the gay village. It's a group program for eating disorders—it runs every Thursday, and they have a session starting on June 11th. I think it'll be good for you."

My throat clenched. "I don't know. It's embarrassing. We all just sit around feeling sorry for ourselves? Sharing stories of puking our guts out?"

He shook his head. "Don't say that. It's comments like that that make people feel ashamed and not want to share."

"Okay. I get that. Sorry."

"Plus, I think it will help you to see that you're not the only person—or guy—dealing with this problem." He gave me that look. The same look that he gave me when he said life didn't owe me anything. "Guess what Tony? This world is huge. You're one person on this planet. One. A pebble."

"Thanks. I feel special."

But he was right.

"I'll probably be the only guy."

"No, you won't. Anyway, what's the harm in trying?"

I tried to joke. "Can't you just prescribe a magic pill that will fix me?"

"No, and that's not funny."

I grimaced.

"And you won't be the only guy, okay?" he said.

Thursday, June 11th. I was the only guy in the group.

The therapy rooms at the Light House were warm. At the front of the room where the group took place was a fireplace; they must've known that people with eating disorders are likely to have low body fat, making them feel cold all the time. Or maybe they were jacking up the heat to force us to take off our jackets, so we'd have a clear view of each other's bodies. I didn't need to be competing against these people to be the skinniest person, or the fattest... I didn't even know what side I'd want to be on.

That was a lie. I did know. And that's what was disturbing.

I didn't want to be there. I wanted to eat, but still be thin.

I didn't want to gain weight.

The thought terrified me. Did that mean I didn't want to get better? That I'd rather stay sick so I could stay skinny? *This isn't normal. Stop thinking.* I reached into my backpack and discreetly slipped a bromazepam in my mouth.

There were three couches, one loveseat and a couple of chairs in a circle. The couches were plush and velvety. I was the second person to arrive. A girl, who looked about 16 years old, sat on the edge of the farthest couch from me. She briefly looked up at me and then immediately down. Maybe she was younger than 16. No makeup on and no scars on her face. Baby skin, clear, unblemished, cream. A big mop of curly brown hair.

Why would somebody that young have to deal with this issue?

I sat down on the other edge of the opposite couch and looked down.

A few minutes later another woman walked in. Mid-thirties, brown hair. Excessive makeup. Michael Kors bag. The bottom of her heels had a red stripe on them.

The room filled up with more women—six of them were white, two were Asian, and one was black. A couple of them looked taken aback when they saw me. I could read it on their faces: "Why is there a guy in here?" With the exemption of one of the Asian girls, they were all pretty thin. But they didn't look as thin as I thought I looked—and for that I felt shamefully proud.

Not normal.

It was two minutes before the scheduled meeting time. I got more and more anxious by the second.

Were any other boys coming?

My running thoughts were interrupted by the sound of heavy boot steps approaching the door.

It was our facilitator, Leslie. She had just finished her master's in social work and this was the second group she had ever led. She looked young and sweet, and skinny as well. My thoughts ran: *How do we know she isn't suffering from the same thing we are? Should we trust her? How can she help us if she can't help herself?*

After introducing herself, she got down to business. "Over the next eight weeks, we're going to help each other to change not only our eating habits, but also our mindset. I want you to be able nourish yourself, get yourself strong and healthy, and learn to eat without anxiety."

She terrified me. I didn't want to get healthy. I didn't want to eat. Food was the enemy. The word "healthy" meant "strong," and "strong" suggested "big"... "thick." I wanted to be thin, light ... invisible.

We went around the room introducing ourselves and explaining why we were here. Everyone's spiel sounded the same—

"My name is Shelley. I'm here because I want to get better."

"I'm Mary. I'm here because I want to be healthy."

—except for one or two eyebrow-raising comments: "I'm April. I'm here because my parents forced me. I guess they got sick of hearing me yack in the bathroom."

This was the young girl who was there when I first walked in.

The other women looked a little shocked.

"It's okay, April. You can say anything you feel comfortable saying. This is a safe place," Leslie said in a calm, measured voice. "That goes for everyone. You can say whatever you want. And I want you to keep in mind that this is a place of mutual respect."

The next person to speak was the Michael Kors bag/red stripped heels: "Hi everyone, I'm Amanda. I'm here because I'm trying to get better. This is my third workshop here. My, I don't know, millionth group since I first had this problem, about twenty years ago. They always say you gotta keep trying until something sticks, right?"

Twenty years she had dealt with this disorder. I couldn't imagine going through this for another year, let alone twenty.

This is why I'm here. So I don't end up like her.

It was my turn. I didn't know what to say. *Just be generic,* I thought. *Be like everyone else, try to be forgettable.* Being the only guy in the room already made me stick out.

"Hi, everyone. I'm Tony. I want to learn how to take better care of myself," I said, staring at my hands.

"Do you feel weird being the only guy?"

I looked up. The room was looking at April, the girl who made the yacking comment earlier.

"You don't need to answer that, Tony," said Leslie.

"It's okay," I said. "I know. It's not very common for guys. Yeah, honestly, I do feel weird. Kinda like the elephant in the room."

"Well, you can't feel that bad, 'cause you're skinnier than the rest of us," April said, completely deadpan.

Dead silence. *Was that a joke?*

It was like April had read my mind. I instantly felt validated.

Validation never came from compliments. It came from comments like that from April, or other voices of concern in my everyday life: "Tony, oh my God, are you okay? You're so thin!" and "Are you sick or something?" If I looked ill, that meant that my efforts to lose weight were succeeding, and that others were envious of my body.

"Okay everyone," Leslie said. "I'm going to get into this in the next few weeks, but I just want to say that April's comment—and April, this isn't me picking on you, or saying you did something wrong—but her compliment about Tony being skinny actually validates and feeds the eating disorder. We're going to work on this again in the future, but for now, I'm just going to call it out whenever it happens."

Leslie had nailed my sick way of thinking. *Maybe she isn't just young and sweet.*

After reviewing meeting times and housekeeping, she gave us the following exercise, which we were to complete for next session:

***

Exercise 1.1: Judging Self-Worth

People with body-image distress tend to judge their self-worth based largely on their shape and weight and their ability to control them. They may have other interests, but over time those take on lesser importance in their lives. This system of self-evaluation can develop through specific life experiences or through the influence of family, friends and the media, or it might just be part of the individual's personality. Over time, they begin to put less and less importance on other measures of worth, as shown in this sample pie chart.

Self-Worth Pie Chart

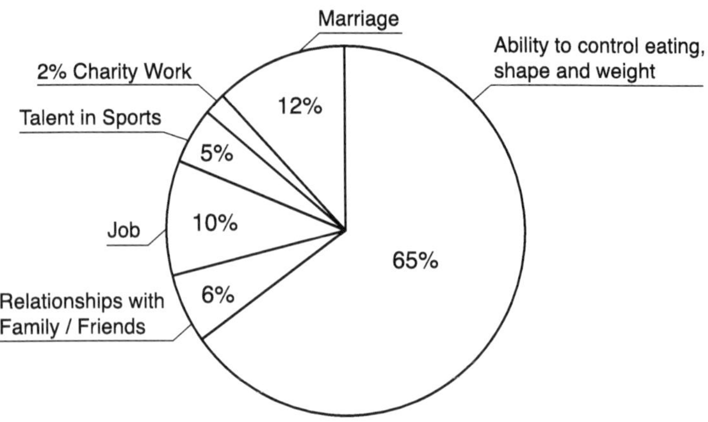

They begin counting on this *one* area of their life to work out for them so that they can be happy and believe in their own worth. When they then struggle to maintain their eating, shape and weight, they judge themselves negatively and think they are of no value.

Your turn:

Create your own chart. How do you judge your self-worth?
List the criteria that make up your self-worth, give each one a
percentage in terms of importance and fill in the circle accordingly.

1. ____

2. ____

3. ____

4. ____

5. ____

6. ____

Chapter 18: Rosalinda

Antonio told me to meet him at his second job the next night at the White Flamingo Bar, at the north end of the village. I invited Nick and Lisa to join—they were always up for getting wasted. And I'd kill two birds with one stone by hanging with them and keeping up the momentum with Antonio. Maximum usage of everyone's time.

This was the second time I'd been out in a bar in the last two months—a rarity. I decided to relax with a rum and Diet Coke. Lisa asked me what was up with Antonio.

"I don't know what it is," I said.

"Come on," she said. "You guys like each other obviously."

"Yeah."

Of course, Nick was never one for subtlety. "Come on, Tone. Let's just get real for a second. You know you want to know what his dick tastes like!"

"Oh my God, Nick. Horrible."

"Come on man! When's the last time you had hole?" he said.

I was about to answer and he interrupted me: "See! If you have to think about it, it's been too long."

We laughed. "Laughing looks good on you, bro," Nick said. "You should do it more often."

"Where's Antonio?" asked Lisa.

"Not sure," I said.

I was a little anxious. What if Nick and Lisa didn't like him? What would I do? I couldn't answer that question. Instead I found myself going back to the bar and ordering another rum and diet.

Suddenly the bar went dark and a loud voice came on the speakers.

"Ladies and Ladies, it's almost midnight ... you know that means!"

Everybody started clapping and howling.

"It's the Flamingo's Best Ass contest—hosted by our very own little taco, Rosalinda!"

The crowd erupted in applause and hollers. A drag queen wearing a tight red dress, red high heels and a blonde wig came out onto the stage.

"Well, hello hello, my little faggots and carpet munchers! How are ya?!" she yelled. The audience laughed and cheered.

Her voice was familiar.

Nick, Lisa and I pushed our way into the crowd, closer to the stage.

Rosalinda wore a tiara. Her face was caked with makeup.

"Ola, senoras and senoritas! I'm Rosalinda and I'll be filling in tonight for your regular host, Miss Dairy Kween! Tonight our top prize is $300 for the best ass plus a round of drinks. And a dance with yours truly."

The crowd began whistling.

I studied her face more. She had light brown, or maybe grey, eyes maybe... Was the rum playing tricks on me?

Suddenly Ben and Kevin came up behind me. "Hey Tony—my A-Gay! Isn't Antonio beautiful up there?"

"What?"

I turned back to the stage and squinted, trying to get a clearer vision. "Oh my God."

It was him.

Antonio. Rosalinda. Same person.

He was stunning—I couldn't decide if he was more attractive as a male or as a female.

"What the fuck? That's Antonio?" Lisa said, laughing. "Tony, his look at his legs! They're gorgeous. And his waist. He's got to be a size 0 or 2. That bitch!"

"Tony, did you know about this? 'Cuz damn, she could turn a fag!" Nick laughed.

"No idea."

I was stunned. How had this not come up over dinner that night? All that talk about art—ugh. Maybe the sugar and syrup seeped into my brain and that detail slipped my mind.

My shock turned to awe the more I looked at him. "He's beautiful, I mean—she's beautiful!" I beamed with pride. "Fucking beautiful. That's my boy!"

"Isn't she amazing?" Ben asked me. "How did you not know this ho did drag? Anyway, she's still new. A bit ratchet, but she's got potential, you know. The people love her. I think they want to make her a regular stand-in when Dairy Kween can't host."

"I need another drink," I said.

"Here you go." Nick handed me something in a martini glass. "Drink baby! It's not every day you find out your trick is a chick!"

Antonio—Rosalinda—was a natural. I barely registered what he was saying; I was still trying to understand how he was able to transform himself so completely. I looked around at the crowd. They stood captivated and hung on her every word.

"Now it's the time get some contestants!" she yelled. "I need three! Come on boys! It's the fastest wad of cash you can make without having to swallow!"

A muscular white man approached the stage. "Right here!" he said.

"All right! Come on up!" Rosalinda said.

The crowd whistled as the man got up on stage.

"Muy bien. What's your name, hon?" She shoved the microphone in his face.

"Homer," he said.

"What? Homo?" Rosalinda said.

"No, Homer."

"Okay, Homo. How old are you and do you have a boyfriend?"

"I'm twenty-six and no, I'm single."

"All right, then let's get you one! Right guys?"

The audience cheered.

"Now turn around and drop your pants!" Rosalinda ordered.

Homer turned around and slowly lowered his jeans, revealing a blue G-string. The crowd got rowdier.

"No honey," Rosalinda said, "we want to see it all! Off with the dental floss!"

Homer laughed, took a deep breath, and pulled down his G-string. The crowd cheered.

"There you have it folks! Let's hear it for Homo! Shake that ass, Homo!" Rosalinda yelled.

The music got louder, and Homer shook his hips and jiggled his butt. The cheeks on his face and butt were the same shade of pale pink.

Somebody lowered the music.

"All right, enough of that white ass. I feel like doing a line of coke now," Rosalinda said, to which the audience erupted into laughter. "Now get to the side of the stage, you poser!"

Homer walked over to the side of the stage, out of the spotlight.

"Who's next, bitches? It's $300 dollars, people! This ain't real life—we just can't hand it over to our white man over here!"

Lisa turned to me, laughing. "Holy crap, Tony, Antonio is amazing at this."

A group of very young men approached the stage. "This guy!" one of them yelled at Rosalinda, pushing one of the boys in front.

"Oh fuck. Who let the toddlers in? Okay, crawl on up here!" Rosalinda said.

He slowly made his way up to the stage, embarrassed. You could feel the older men salivating, ready to bite.

"Now," Rosalinda said, "what's your name, Baby Jane?"

"Lloyd," he said.

"And how old are you Lloyd?"

"Nineteen."

"Nineteen. Well, aren't you precious!" Rosalinda turned to the audience. "Sorry, my pedophiles, this one's legal. You'll have to go across the street to the daycare if you want to get arrested."

Crowd laughter.

"Now, baby Lloyd, turn around and drop the diapers!"

Lloyd turned around and dropped his pants. He wasn't wearing any underwear. The music got louder as he grinded forward and back.

"Oh, you little slut Lolita! You need a spanking. Bad boy!" Rosalinda said as she slapped Lloyd's butt cheek. "Gentlemen, I think we need a diaper change stat!"

"I'll change that diaper!" some old man from the crowd yelled.

"Sold, to the pervert with the creepy pornstache," Rosalinda said. "All right, Twinky. Go wait at the side of the stage with Homo. And don't let him touch your lollipop."

Rosalinda turned back to the audience. "I need one more, guys! One more! $300 dollars!"

A few seconds went by. Nobody volunteered. Rosalinda walked from the other side of the stage toward us. I always complained about being short, but at this moment I didn't feel short enough. I looked at the ground.

"You!" Rosalinda said.

"Tony," Lisa said.

Fuck. Fuck. No.

I looked up to see Antonio's beautiful eyes piercing at me. "Yes, I'm talking to you, handsome," she said.

"No way!" I yelled.

"I know you, right?" Rosalinda said.

"No, you don't."

"Yeah I do. You're ... you're sexy!" Rosalinda said with a big smile on her face.

"Yeah, get him up there!" I turned around; Nick was smirking and Lisa was trying to encourage me.

Rosalinda bent down and put her hand out to me. I shook my head. "No," I mouthed to her.

She lowered her mouth to my ear. "Don't worry, babe. Trust me." She grabbed my hand and pulled me onstage. My face was on fire. I heard Lisa, Nick, Ben and Kevin cheering for me.

I saw Antonio wink at the tech man the back of the room. He gave her a thumbs up.

"Now honey. What's your name?" Rosalinda asked.

"Tony," I said. My voice cracked. The crowd laughed.

"Tony, honey, have you gone through puberty yet?" Rosalinda asked. Giggles.

"Now how old are you, Tony?"

"Uh. Thirty-four."

Antonio raised an eyebrow and lowered the microphone away from his mouth.

"Really?" he said.

"Yeah," I said. "You never asked me before."

She raised the microphone back to her mouth and smiled. "That's hot." She turned back to the crowd.

"Well, we've got a daddy here, folks!" the crowd whistled. "Are you ready for your deathbed, grandpa? ... I'm kidding, I'm kidding!"

I looked up to see bunch of television monitors in the corners of the bar. The usual porn videos had been replaced by live footage of Rosalinda standing beside some idiot on the stage.

She took my hand and squeezed it. "I'm just yanking ya, honey. I'm older than fucking Cher! Here, touch my face, honey, I'm shellacked more than an Easter egg."

I put my hand up to Rosalinda's face. She swatted it away.

"Oh no, I was just kidding, honey. You'll break me!"

The lights went a bit dimmer.

"All jokes aside," Rosalinda said, "can we applaud Queen Tony for looking so young?"

The crowd cheered and whistled. Antonio winked at me. I relaxed a little.

"Now, it's time!" Rosalinda said.

I shook my head. "I got stretch marks on my ass!" I blurted into the microphone.

The audience burst into laughter.

"Honey, I got stretchmarks in my ass!" Rosalinda turned to the crowd again. "Now who doesn't have stretch marks on their ass here tonight?" The crowed whistled and cheered again.

The next moments were a blur. For once I was hoping I might faint of hunger. I was terrified all over again.

I remember turning around, and Antonio helping take my pants down. I was wearing blue superman boxer briefs. The crowd yelled "Take 'em off!"

Thank God I wasn't facing the crowd, so I couldn't can't see their faces. I started to pull the briefs down, when all of a sudden the lights started flickering on and off, and everything took on a stop-motion feel. Antonio grabbed my underwear with one hand and yanked them lower. I heard some laughter. I wanted to throw up.

Rosalinda screamed into the microphone: "Can we get some love for our Tony here?!"

The music pulsed even faster and louder, accompanying the

strobe lights.

I heard a piercing scream combined with a deep "Yeah, baby! Woohoo!" from the crowd. I looked out—it was Lisa and Nick. Soon Kevin and Ben joined in. Then the whole crowd cheered.

"That's right guys, let's show our appreciation for this brave guy," Rosalinda yelled. The crowd cheered more. Antonio came close to my face and kissed me on the cheek, just like he'd done in the car.

Just then, I remembered how I used to go the clubs all the time when I first came out. How I'd dance on speakers up high and not give a shit what people thought of me, even though I was a lot heavier then.

So, I decided to own it. It may have been the two rum-and-Diets. Or the fact that Antonio was holding my hand. I took it to the extreme. I grinded hard, and the audience loved it. If I was old and embarrassing, then I was going to be the best old and embarrassing contestant ever.

I felt a snap in my thighs. My body suddenly felt heavy. My legs gave out underneath me. I felt the back of my head hit the stage floor.

Thirty minutes later, I sat at the bar, holding an ice pack to my head. Kevin and Ben stumbled toward me. They reeked of sweat and alcohol.

"Hey, Mr. Best Ass," Ben said.

"Mr. Second-Best Ass," I said.

"Whatever," Kevin said. "You would have won if you didn't over-twerk yourself."

I laughed. "That's okay. Thanks for cheering for me on guys."

"You fainted at the Meat Locker last time too, right? Is everything okay?"

"It's fine. Probably just the alcohol."

"Ha-ha. You want some E?" Ben said, holding out a little pill in his hand.

"No. I'm fine. But thanks for offering," I said. "Does your mother know you're taking that shit?"

"You're so sweet," Ben said. "Now, where's Antonio... excuse me, where's that Rosalinda ho?"

"Not sure," I said. "In the bathroom?"

"Okay, we gotta get going. It's a school night," Kevin said.

"Okay. You guys aren't driving, are you?" I asked.

"We're fine," Kevin said. "I have my car."

Stupid fucking children. I'm too old for this. "No. Do you guys have any money? Ugh never mind," I said. I grabbed Kevin's car keys. "You're taking a cab." I reached into my pocket and handed him two twenty dollar bills.

"Thank you, Daddy," Kevin said.

"Yes, thank you, Daddy," Ben said.

"Ha-ha, funny."

"I'm the only one who can call him Daddy, okay bitches?" Antonio entered the circle, still dressed as Rosalinda. "Now go away, you ugly step sisters... shoo, shoo." He waved Kevin and Ben away. "I'll call you guys tomorrow."

Antonio turned back to me. "Where are Nick and Lisa?"

"They went home already."

"Already?"

"Once you pass thirty, you turn into a pumpkin before midnight."

"Enough with the old thing," Antonio said. "I'm really proud of you Tony. You really let yourself loose tonight."

"Yeah. Bared my ass and fell on my head. It was fun," I smirked.

Antonio leaned in, took the ice bag from my hand and put it on the counter. "So can I finally have a dance with you?" he asked.

"Nah," I said. "I'm kinda tired."

"Excuse me? What are we, some boring straight people?"

"Okay, sure. Just be gentle, my hip hurts."

Antonio took me by the hand and led me to the crowded dance floor. It was 1:30 a.m. I couldn't believe I was still out and pretty awake. I felt … young. But then I didn't recognize the dance song that was playing.

We found a spot beside the group of young guys we saw earlier. Lloyd was wearing a gold paper crown on his head and the Best Ass sash over his shirt.

Even with high heels on, Antonio could out-dance them all. He moved so easily and gracefully over the heavy beating music.

The fast beat ended and a slow song began. It had kind of a bluesy, jazz sound to it. The crowd took it as a cue to leave the floor and get more drinks. Soon Antonio and I were standing awkwardly across from each other in the empty space.

"I guess we should head out soon," I said.

As I made to turn away, his hand grabbed mine and he pulled me back to the dance floor, under a spotlight.

Under all that makeup and the blonde wig were those same beautiful eyes and wide smile.

"I want my dance," he said into my ear, determined. He placed my hands on his hips and started swaying me back and forth.

"You were amazing up there," I said. "I had no idea."

"Thanks."

"I don't know how you do it. Don't you get nervous?" I asked.

"Honey, please. I only go to places where I'm elevated … where I can be seen. It's partly about being high up, but it's mostly about me."

I laughed. "God, I love—" I stopped.

Antonio smiled. "Me too."

He put his hands on my shoulders and pulled my head in closer. Soon our noses were almost touching, and I could feel myself drowning in his eyes. That sweet smell of cake returned. The disco lights intermittently flashed across his face and they spun from one side of the room to the other. He put his head down and rested his cheek on my shoulder as we rocked back and forth.

"My house is a bit messy," I said, opening the door for Antonio. I glanced in my reflection in the window to make sure I could see the shadows of my cheekbones. No, I'm supposed to stop doing that—"self-checking," Leslie would call it. I looked away.

I turned on the hallway light.

"What a cute house," Antonio said. "How can it be messy when it's so minimal and uncluttered?"

What a sweetheart he was. "Minimal" and "uncluttered" were kind words to describe my home. I had two small loveseats in my living room—one was black leather, purchased after I'd saved a couple of my Melo paycheques, the other a grey fabric, a Salvation Army find—but there were no pictures, paintings, or plants. The house was a scene of greys and blacks framed in cold white walls.

"Why do you have newspaper on the mirror?" Antonio asked, looking at the closet doors.

Shit. I forgot.

I tore the newspapers down. Each rip revealed more of our reflection, Antonio standing behind me. I looked away—I didn't want to see what we looked like in the same frame.

"I was planning to do some painting and didn't want to dirty the mirrors. Just ignore it." That was the best I could come up with. I thought it was pretty good considering how tipsy I was.

"You don't have any decorations or anything," he said.

"It's just easier to keep it clean."

That was only partly true. It was easier with less stuff around to clean.

I used to have photos of my mom in frames everywhere. But as time went on, I'd put them all in boxes to stop reminding myself of her. Every remnant of her—the curtains she chose, the dusty rose sofa set, the peach lampshades—was gone.

In front of the loveseats was a television that my uncle gave me when he upgraded to something larger. I rarely turned it on. But when I did, I liked to watch movies set outdoors in a foreign country, so I'd at least feel like I had taken a vacation every so often.

Behind the television was a mirror on the wall—also covered in newspaper, which I promptly ripped off in front of Antonio—that I used as a reminder not to binge while watching TV. If I saw myself doing it, I needed to change the image, like changing the channel. No, don't want to see that.

Past the living room was the kitchen. Antonio scanned the white cupboards, the laminate countertops made to look like marble, the linoleum floors with a light pink and mint green faux tile.

"Pardon me," I said. "The 90s died in this house." Along with Mom, and other things. I didn't say that.

I caught Antonio glancing at the overflowing stack of envelopes on my dining table.

"I don't spend much time at home, that's why it looks like I'm just passing through here," I said.

I didn't remember putting the mail there. Depression (or was it anxiety? probably both) placed my mail on the dining table every day, until the pile began to topple over to one side. Then, another pile was created. They—depression and anxiety, that is—never allowed me to open any of the envelopes for fear of what overdue bills lurked inside. At least I managed to toss the flyers into the recycling.

I grabbed the stack of envelopes and tossed them into a cupboard.

The last time I had been with anyone was six years before with Ken, prior to me dropping all the weight. I always made sure the lights were off before I undressed. At least I was thinner now, so if that opportunity presented itself, I'd feel comfortable keeping a lamp on. Not that it mattered. Much of gay Toronto had already seen my ass shake itself out of control.

Antonio put his hands gently to the sides of my face, like in some movie, and kissed me. I could smell the sweetness coming off his skin. He was a great kisser.

"Antonio."

"Yeah."

"Can I ask you a weird question?"

"Shoot."

"Why do you always smell like cake?"

He chuckled. "It's my lotion. It's called birthday cake suit. Do you not like it?"

"No, I love it actually. Makes me wanna eat you."

He stepped back and peeled his shirt off, revealing the sinews of his muscles that flexed from his golden-brown skin. Then he reached out and pulled my shirt over my head.

He stopped. His smile faded as he scanned from my shoulders to my chest to my stomach.

"What?" I said.

He didn't say anything.

"What?" I repeated.

"I can see your ribs. I guess I never realized how skinny you were."

Usually, this type of comment would boost my confidence.

"Tony. Are you okay?"

"Yeah, of course. I'm fine."

His eyes kept travelling over my body. I tried to get them back to my face. "I'm fine. Never mind. Just come here and kiss me." I planted my face on his.

We moved to the bedroom and fell onto my bed, where we rolled around until we were both naked.

"You ready?" I asked.

"As long as you are."

"You have a condom?"

"Yeah."

I flipped on my stomach as he grabbed a condom from his backpack. I heard him fiddling with the package. "Shit," he said.

I turned around. His hands were shaking trying to get the condom on. "You need help?"

"No. I got it."

"Okay." I turned back over.

"Just relax," he said.

He pressed his hips toward my lower back, and I felt him slowly start to enter. It felt massive; immediately I clenched.

Perhaps it was his size. Or maybe I was too nervous. Then I remembered—in the last few days, I had overdone it with the laxatives, which had given me bad diarrhea; I'd ended up bleeding back there. Cleaning myself with toilet paper since then had been torture.

And trying to jam a seven-inch object into that same hole probably wasn't helping.

"Are you okay, Tony? You're crazy tight," he said, sounding concerned.

"Yeah I'm fine. Keep going."

"Okay."

He slowly entered again, repeatedly asking if I was okay. I felt the sting of my skin ripping. Pain shot up my back.

"Does that hurt?"

"No, I'm fine. Keep going."

He slowed down.

"Antonio, I'm fine. Don't worry." It hurt so bad. My whole body tightened. I closed my eyes and tried to breathe through it.

"You don't sound fine. You sound like you're in pain, like I'm attacking you," Antonio said.

I laughed it off. "Don't' worry, I'm into S and M. Just go."

Antonio didn't find it funny. He started again, going slower and slower, until he pulled out. "Fuck."

"You okay?" I asked.

"I'm sorry."

I turned around and saw him jerking himself. "I lost it. I'm sorry. I'm soft."

"Oh. Okay. Is it me? I'm so sorry."

"No it's not you. Well ..."

I knew it was me.

He continued. "I'm scared I'm hurting you. I feel like I'm going to break you."

"You won't."

"Do you wanna try topping me?"

I had only tried topping once or twice before, right when I came out. But as the dosage of my antidepressants increased over the years, I'd found it more and more difficult to maintain an erection.

"I'm sorry, I guess I'm a bit tired." I could hear the embarrassment in my voice.

He conceded as well. "It's okay, honey. I have to get up early for class tomorrow anyway."

He lay down and spooned me, embracing my arms, then my chest, and finally resting his hands on my stomach, rubbing it as if I were a child. He squeezed me tightly and kissed the back of my neck.

Disaster. I had lost the weight thinking it would make me attractive. Now I'd finally found a guy but my new body couldn't stand the pain enough to keep him interested.

"Can I ask you something?" I said.

"Of course."

"Am I ... missing something?"

"What do you mean?"

"Why do you like me?"

"What kind of fucking question is that?"

"I'm not sure why you like me. Aren't you too hot for me?"

"You're ridiculous."

"It's true."

He sighed. "Well ... I can't believe you're making me do this. I like you because you're kind. You're funny, even though I know you're sad sometimes. You ask me questions about myself, even though you have something else way more important on your mind. You always wait for me to finish talking when I'm rambling. You can recite poems off the top of your head. I like you because you're a great teacher. You really connect with the kids—they love you, you know? I don't know why you work at that office—you should stick to teaching." He paused. "And, oh yeah, I kind of have a thing for Bruno Mars," he laughed. "Is that a good enough answer for you?"

"Yeah." I was somewhat appeased. I rolled over to face him. "Do you want to know why I like you?"

I could rhyme off a million things. The way his eyes pulled anyone in. The way he was so comfortable—no, comfortable wasn't the right word—the way he embraced his beautifully sweet and femmie self. How talented an artist he was. How he made me realize that all millennials weren't stupid and basic. How his personality could light up any room, remarkably matching his striking looks.

"No, I don't wanna know why you like me," he said.

"No?"

"If you like me, then that's all that matters. Let's not overthink it."

I didn't sleep that night. I drifted in and out of hazy clouds of shame, because of the sex (or lack thereof)—and because of my relief, realizing he'd stayed the night anyway.

Chapter 19: The Secret to Happiness

I had never been one to claim I knew everything, or that anything was 100% certain—but that night I lay in bed next to Antonio, thinking about one thing that I'd learned to be true.

The secret to happiness was to lower expectations.

This hadn't come from some TED Talk, or an episode of Oprah. I'd figured it out all by myself. Of course, I'd heard variations of it in books or on TV:

"Be realistic."

"Reassess your goals and see if they are really feasible."

"Shoot for the moon, even if you miss, you'll be among the stars."

Really, it was all the same thing—no need to sugar coat.

Everybody had gotten too sensitive. If your goal to was to make $80,000 annually in your job, then you should expect to make $50,000. If you wanted to marry a woman who was a "10", settle for a "6". If you wanted to be a doctor, aim for nursing.

I felt like people were always underestimating the damage disappointments could do to them. The expectation to have both of my parents around, to grow old with my mom, to graduate from university, all ended in failure and disappointment: Dad had left, Mom had died, and I'd flunked my way out of the university before first year ended. Had I not expected everything to be normal, that my family would be around for a while or that I'd succeed at U of T as my high-school performance had predicted, maybe I wouldn't have been left so dumbfounded and crippled when it all came crashing down. That was the problem—expectations.

Or maybe the key to happiness was resilience. A method of defence. Disappointment was inevitable—we just had to keep bouncing back. But being resilient wasn't a quality someone just had, was it? Were people born resilient? Could we learn it? Hopefully. Otherwise, my expectation of being happy by developing resilience would only end up in disappointment. What a vicious cycle I'd just uncovered! This was unexpected—thus, I had achieved happiness. Cue the fucking conga line.

I cleverly brought up this pearl of wisdom the morning after finding out Antonio was also Rosalinda, bringing him home, and *not* having sex with him.

"Geeze, you are so cynical," he said, lying on my couch in front of the television. I felt the difference in our ages. "The secret to happiness is not lowering expectations. It's looking forward to something. Having hope that something better in the future is possible, and working toward it," he said.

"Until you get disappointed," I said, bursting his bubble.

He rolled his eyes. "You tell the kids at Gold's to follow their dreams. You're so full of shit. Whatever." He got up and walked to the window overlooking the backyard. "Who does the gardening?" he asked.

The backyard was an embarrassment. The grass had dried out to yellow and brown, and weeds were scattered everywhere. As expected, I hadn't taken care of my mother's roses. They hung over, dried out, most of the petals having fallen off to the dirt, like corpses drifting with their heads cut off.

"My mom did. It's what made her happy. I've been shit at maintaining it since she died. I tried, but the flowers just weren't as big or red anymore. So I gave up.”

Antonio continued to stare out the window.

Chapter 20: The Light House, Session 3

I'd read somewhere that some men suffered from eating disorders on the opposite side of the spectrum from me. Instead of starving, or bingeing and purging, they obsessed with gaining as much muscle mass as possible, compulsively working out, eating abnormally large amounts of protein, and in some cases taking steroids. They wanted the numbers on their scales to be as large as possible, which boggled my mind. I figured that these guys were just alpha males preoccupied with not seeming small, weak, feminine—a case of hypermasculinity rearing its ugly head once again—but Dr. Tee told me that's not always true. Rather, some of these men were driven by the same basic insecurity that drove me—that they weren't good enough as they were. So it seemed that in my feminine skinny Asian-ness, I had the same neuroses—fear, envy, obsession etc.—as these guys. But where they strived for the stereotypical strong and sturdy male physique, I rejected it.

My thoughts were interrupted by Leslie: "How did everyone do with this week's activity?"

Nobody replied. This was our third session, and people still did not feel comfortable to speak unless called on.

"Okay," Leslie said, "how about we start by taking out last week's worksheets."

I reached into my backpack and pulled out the folded papers.

***

Exercise 4.3: Body Checking / Body Avoidance

Frequency Scale

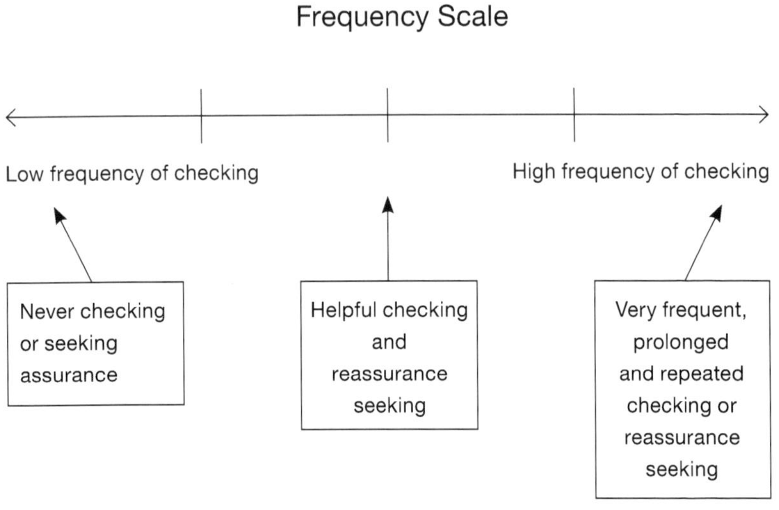

Identify the areas of your body that you check/avoid and how you are doing this (in mirror, with hands, with clothing, etc.)

•

•

•

Estimate the time you spend/amount of times doing these things on a daily basis.

•

•

•

Think about specific situations where you might be more activated to body check or body avoid (while with others, while alone, after a meal, before a meal, etc.)

-
-
-

What are your thoughts while you check/avoid your body?

-
-
-

***

Homework

Choose three behaviours and try to stop (don't do it), limit (do it once a day instead of throughout, or only at a certain time) or reduce (try to gradually reduce your behaviour) them. Keep track of the situations you are in when you are triggered to body check/avoid and how you are feeling at the time. Try other coping strategies and track how your distress changes over time.

<u>Step 1: Evaluate how helpful your current behaviour is</u>

Current behaviour:

____

____

Advantages of current behaviour:

____

____

Disadvantages of current behaviour:

____

____

Does it make sense to continue with this behaviour?

____

____

Step 2: Generate and evaluate a new behavioural goal

New behaviour:

____

____

Advantages of new behaviour:

____

____

Disadvantages of current behaviour:

____

____

Does it make sense to continue with this new behaviour?

____

____

"Tony, your worksheets are blank," Leslie said to me.

"I know. I'm sorry. It was a crazy week, and I just didn't have time to try this one out," I said.

"That's okay. Try for next week, okay?"

"Thanks."

I was lying. I did try out the body-checking/body-avoidance exercise. I was too ashamed to talk about the results.

"Anybody else want to share?" Leslie asked the group.

Another few seconds of silence.

"I'll go," Amanda said.

"Okay great," Leslie said enthusiastically.

"So, I decided I was going to count how many times I looked in the mirror. I accounted for all the times I looked in the mirrors in my house, the ones at the office, the one in the train washroom. The rear-view mirror and cosmetic mirror in my car. And of course, the compact in my purse."

"That's great," Leslie said.

A few people in the group leaned in, looking really interested. Others, like April, looked like she couldn't have cared less. Or like she really didn't want to be in group today. Or both.

Amanda continued. "I kept a little notebook in my purse and jotted down how many times I checked any mirror for a week."

"And what were your results?" Leslie asked.

"125 times on Monday. 113 on Tuesday. 187 on Wednesday. I'm guessing it spiked that day because I had a huge presentation at work. I checked my mirror a bunch of times that morning because I couldn't decide on what to wear for it. Usually takes me forever to do this every day—to choose my clothes, I mean—but on Wednesday it took me almost an hour to finally decide and leave the house. I ended up being late for it."

A few of the women nodded, seemingly familiar with that situation.

"You said you spent about an hour that morning choosing what you were going to wear?" Leslie asked.

"Yeah."

"How many different outfits did you try?"

"Oh my God. Like seven different blazers, five shirts, eight pairs of pants," Amanda said. "At least I didn't also have to try on dresses and skirts. I never wear anything that would draw any attention to my legs; they're disgusting."

Everybody looked down at her legs. I tried to be discreet about it. Her legs were thin, just like the rest of her.

"Amanda, do you know why you keep checking the mirror so much?" Leslie asked.

"I don't know. Because I'm crazy? I think maybe I'll see someone different the next time. Someone that doesn't repulse me." She shook her head.

"Amanda, I want you to know … actually all of you should know that mirrors are not true reflections of what you really look like. Do you guys ever notice that in some mirrors you look great, and in others, not so much? On top of that, you have your own biases, your judgments of yourselves, that refract or distort the image. What you in see in the mirror can be completely different from what others see," Leslie said.

"I'm sorry I'm so negative," Amanda said. She changed her tone of voice. "So, anyway, for the exercise, I'd try to do a different activity every time I had the urge to look into the mirror. So I decided that I'd check my phone. Check what's happening with Facebook or Instagram, whatever."

"And how'd that go?" Leslie asked.

"It was okay. I only checked the mirror about eighty times that first day, then maybe sixty-five the next one."

"That's great," one of the group members said.

"Do you think this is something you can sustain? Perhaps you could even make it a goal to keep decreasing that number?" Leslie said.

"Well, I don't know. I went over my data on my phone bill. I had to fork out an extra $50 this month." Some of the group members laughed. "Maybe I need to find a new replacement behaviour."

"Well you're definitely on the right track," Leslie said. "Replacement behaviours are important, but maybe checking your phone isn't the best idea. Social media can trigger you to compare yourself to others, which can lead to more problems."

Some people wrote this down in their notebooks.

"Now, anyone else want to share? How about you, April?"

April pulled out a textbook from her backpack—"Advanced Calculus"—and rifled through some loose papers inside the cover.

"Here it is." She looked around the room warily.

"It's okay, April," Leslie said. "No need to feel shy. Remember what I said about this being safe space for everyone. Nobody is going to judge you."

April cleared her throat. "Um, okay so I know I weigh myself on the scale way too much. So for few days I counted how many times I was doing it."

"Okay, great."

"It was like close to fifty times a day. About fifteen times in the morning before going to school. As soon as I get out of bed, after I take a shower, clothes off, clothes on. Then as soon as I get home. Before doing my homework, after doing my homework. Even during homework, like as a study break, I'd just weigh myself."

"I understand. And what are you thinking when you are doing it?"

"That I can't go over a certain number. But it doesn't make sense. Sometimes I'll weigh more an hour after not eating anything."

"And what do you do if you see a number you don't like?"

"I go for a walk to burn some calories. If the weather is bad, I'll do sit-ups in my bedroom."

"Are your parents aware of any of this?"

"Yeah. Well, sort of, I guess."

"They know?"

"Yeah. I had this problem last year ... they kept catching me doing sit-ups. Then eventually my dad said he heard me creeping in and out of the bathroom to get to the scale. I told my parents I had irritable bowel syndrome, and that's why I always had to go. But then one time I brought the scale to my bedroom, and my mom walked in while I was standing on it. She told my dad, and then he threw the scale out. I went out and bought another one from Walmart with my debit card and kept it under my bed. My parents found that one and threw it out too. I got another one that I'm hiding at the back of my closet. I have to tip toe and be real quiet when I use it. They'll kill me if they find out."

The room was silent.

I had an appointment with Dr. Tee the next evening.

"I don't know if this group is for me," I said.

"Why is that?" Dr. Tee asked.

"Some of the exercises—I don't think they're working."

"Yes, that's CBT for you," he said.

"I don't feel any changes."

"You need to give it time. The idea behind CBT is that as you repeat certain behaviours, like food logging or replacement activities, your thoughts will change with the behaviour. If you change something you do, like every time you want to binge, you instead go for a walk, or read, or do another activity in replacement, your brain will start to automatically not want to binge and do the new activity instead."

"I'm sorry, but sometimes I just think a lot of it is bullshit."

"Tony, you need to go into this with an open attitude," Dr. Tee said.

"You know what they made us do last week?"

"What?"

"This body-checking exercise. Some of us decided to count how many times we looked in the mirror for the week. I counted almost 100 times the first day. That doesn't even count the times I see myself in any sort of shiny surface—a store window, a glass door .... It only made me aware of how nuts I was. Do you know what I ended up doing at home?" I asked.

"What?"

"I ended up covering the all the mirrors in my house with newspaper. I couldn't stand to keep counting how many times I checked. Couldn't stand to even look at myself anymore, just the same stupid fat face. I didn't share my experience with the group, I was too embarrassed."

Dr. Tee took a breath and leaned back into his chair. "I don't know what to say. Maybe you could try another group?"

I rolled my eyes.

"Tony."

"Yeah?"

"There's also an inpatient program at St. Paul's hospital. I want you to think about it. You would stay there—in the hospital—for about three months. You'd have counselling, classes, stay with other patients. They'd get you on a regular eating schedule."

"What do you mean *regular* eating schedule?"

"You eat three meals a day. And they force you to keep it in. You can't use the bathroom for a certain time after eating."

My throat clenched. "No, not an option."

Chapter 21: Cloud Cover

I let out Saturday's writing class about fifteen minutes early, closed my classroom, and went to Antonio's class. He saw me peeking in the door and called to me in front of the students: "Hey stranger, come in, take seat in the back." I quickly sat myself in an empty chair near the door. Some students smiled at me and waved.

"Actually, why don't we have Tony participate in today's exercise? You all know him, right?" Antonio said to the students.

"Yeah!" said Taylor, the one from my weeknight classes.

"Okay, sure," I said.

Antonio gestured for me to come to the front. "So we were just doing some critiques of last week's assignment, which was abstract art. So Tony, I'm going to get you to do a critique."

"I don't know much about abstract art or critiques."

"That doesn't matter. We're not snotty artists in this class, are we guys?" Antonio reassured me as he looked around the room. "John, come up here with your piece."

John—the same boy who wrote about his father in my weeknight classes—came to the front with a with large canvas of blue, white and grey swirls.

"What did you call this piece, John?" Antonio asked.

"Cloud Cover," John replied.

Antonio looked at me. "Okay, Tony, what does this piece make you think of, or say to you? Anything that comes into your head."

"Well," I started, "it's really cool, John."

"Thanks," John said.

"Okay, but beyond platitudes, Tony. What else about it? What does it make you think or feel?" Antonio asked.

I scanned the painting from top to bottom and then side to side.

The first thing that came into my head was something Leslie said at the Light House. *Thoughts are like passing clouds.* But I didn't say that out loud.

I tried my best to sound like some sort of art critic. "The brush strokes are really loose and it looks like you painted pretty quickly. I like how the colours blend into each other seamlessly so that I can't tell where the clouds end the sky begins. I also like how the mood of it is really calming, and a bit sombre. It looks like you just let your mood lead the way instead of your eyes."

"Not bad, Tony," Antonio said, "great critique." He turned to John. "Now John, can you tell us anything you want us to know about the painting, or how you interpret it?"

"There's not much to interpret," John replied. "I was just outside waiting for the sun to come out so I could paint a bright sky. But it never came. So I just went with what was there."

After class, the room emptied.

"Thanks for joining in on the class. I kinda put you on the spot there," Antonio said.

"Sure. Anything for the kids."

He leaned in and kissed me on the lips. "You're the best. What are you doing here anyway?"

"I wanted to take you to Fran's for pancakes, and then somewhere special," I said. "Go get your stuff."

"Do I really have to wear this stupid blindfold?" Antonio asked. We had just finished lunch, where he grilled me on where I was taking him afterward.

"We're almost there," I said as I drove. "Keep that blindfold on!"

Eventually, he let go of my hand and hugged my arm like a child. "This is either going to be super kinky, like you're going to screw me blindfolded in a forest, or super scary, like you're going to screw me blindfolded in a forest and then chop my head off with an axe."

"You spoiled the surprise!"

"We could just stop driving now and you can do me here in the car. No need to be so dramatic, Tones!"

"Oh, shut up. I'm too old for car sex."

I pulled up to our destination and led him toward the entrance. "Almost there," I said. "Just a few more steps."

We stopped. "Okay, Miss Rosalinda. Surprise!" I pulled his blindfold off.

He scanned the building in front of us. "We're at the Art Gallery?"

"Yup. The AGO."

"Oh neat. Are we going in?"

"Yeah. They're showcasing this Swedish artist... Klimp?"

"I know," Antonio interrupted. "Gustav Klimt. He's Austrian. I love him."

"Give me your hand."

"Okay." Antonio extended his hand to me. I reached into my pocket, pulled out a card and placed it in his palm. He lifted the card to examine it.

"A membership? You got me a membership?" he asked.

"Yeah. If you donate a certain amount, you become a member for a whole year, so I did it on your behalf. You can come here whenever you want."

"What? No. IRL?"

"What the fuck is IRL?"

"In real life!"

"Oh. Yeah. In real life."

His face melted into a smile, all teeth and dimples, raised eyebrows and big eyes. "Holy shit, Tony, thank you! Thank you so much! I don't know what to say... this is the best gift, like ever. Oh my God!"

"Who's yo Daddy?!" I smirked. I thought this was witty since I'd never imagined myself to be anyone's sugar daddy. Not on my salary.

We laughed as he picked me up off the ground and twirled me around as he pressed his lips against mine. I could see the shadows of my feet swirling faster and faster, while people in the corners of my eyes stopped and watched. I wondered if the girls in romantic comedies got dizzy in these kinds of moments.

I don't know if it was the spinning, or the blinding sun, or the feeling of being lifted and spun by Antonio, but at that moment I decided I would take Dr. Tee's advice. I was going to do every CBT exercise given to me, whether I believed it was going to work or not.

Chapter 22: Number 1

Lauren had been tasked with preparing our finances for our annual audit at Melo. Since I'd worked on our financial reporting for the last couple of years, she asked me to assist. I mainly helped with gathering the sources of our numbers and walking her through our systems. She then was able to take the results and present them in a PowerPoint deck that looked like it was done by a graphic artist, an amazing upgrade from my boring bar graphs in Excel.

Jell-O was pleased with our work.

"These are top drawer, Laur. Comprehensive, clear and super slick. Great work."

"It wasn't me, Victor. Tony compiled and explained the data to me. I was completely lost without him," Lauren said.

I smiled. "Thanks Lauren. It was a team effort."

Jell-O nodded, smiling at me. "All right, excellent Tony! Onwards and upwards, guys!"

"Really Tony, I owe you a drink," Lauren said at the end of the day. "I could not have done that without you."

"All good. I remember when I had to work the auditing crap the first time. I was totally confused."

"Getting the numbers to jive was killer. You were amazing."

"Thanks."

I had worked for hours late into a couple of nights on those spreadsheets, even cancelling a dinner with Antonio once. The spreadsheets were incredibly complex, and I got stressed to the point that I wanted to binge, but I was able to restrain myself by using a technique from one of the Light House group members, which was *not* focusing on how high I would feel off the food, but rather on how terrible I would feel after purging. The process of reasoning it out prevented me from doing it; it was a small victory, but a victory nonetheless.

"You have any plans tonight?" Lauren asked.

"No. Just dinner with a couple of my friends in the village. How about yourself?"

"Going to go meet some friends for coffee at the Starbucks." She picked up her Lululemon bag to head out the door. "I'll walk you—I'm going in your direction."

I was usually too exhausted for small talk. The walk to Le Jardin was supposed to be my resting time. "Sure," I said, with a smile.

"No worries if not Tony. If you want to relax and have alone time on the way home, I totally get that." She sounded genuine.

I chuckled. "Shit, do I look like that much of a bitch?"

She smiled. "No, no, oh God, that's not what I mean."

"No worries. I'm kidding."

"I mean, if you don't want to just detach from work on your way, it's all good. Or if you feel it's going to be awkward. I get social anxiety too."

"Wow, you're really direct. No, it's fine. We can just walk in silence and acknowledge that silence is okay, and not awkward."

"Okay. Let's do that. I'm glad we talked about it first. After you."

Whenever Lauren walked, her ponytail bounced from side to side. It made me think she was this young (well, she was young), hopeful optimist.

"So, are you one of those Starbucks addicts who gets a venti mocha choco latte for eight bucks a day?" I asked her.

"Oh no. More like a short regular. I can't afford it."

"Oh, sorry, I assumed. I see all you young'uns hanging around the little hipster coffee shops after work all the time, ordering organic or free trade or whatever."

"No, that's not really me. Although I do compost."

"Excellent."

"Actually, I go to this Starbucks every Tuesday and Thursday night to meet my boyfriend and another friend. We go over to Ryerson for our classes at six-thirty."

"What classes?"

"Pre-CPA courses. We go over our homework and then head to class. Fun times."

I realized that after months of working with her, even becoming her assistant in a way—although she never made me feel like it—I barely knew Lauren.

"You're doing your CPA? Jesus. Aren't you tired? Jell-O's got you working like a dog, especially since all my work came to you."

"Jell-O?"

Shit.

"Melo. I mean Melo. Victor."

"I am tired. I volunteer on Monday nights too."

"You do? Where?"

"At the mental health clinic on Queen. I do admin work, sometimes call patients with appointment reminders. Puts it all into perspective. And I can't lie ... it does help the resume too."

"You're nuts. You're going to burn out."

"Yeah, but it makes me think it'll amount to something. Not to offend you, Tony... you know what, never mind."

"What?"

"No, I don't want to offend you. It's dumb."

"There's no way you can offend me. Seriously tell me."

She shook her head. "Ok, now this is awkward. Let's have just have an awkward silence."

"Seriously?"

"Okay fine. I just... I don't want to stay at Melo and Co. forever, you know. I want to move out of my parents' house one day."

"I get that."

"I want to afford rent. I want to be able to own a car. I don't even care what kind. A Corolla? Those are cheap, right? Nowadays, the minimum is a CPA, or an MBA, or anything to show you're that special snowflake that the company needs to hire."

I was going to tell her to lower her standards, but she seemed to already know that.

She continued. "When you go for these job interviews, it doesn't matter if you come second, or third or whatever. There's only one job. So you *have* to be number one. Every other place is useless. Like you shouldn't have even bothered."

"Do you even like accounting?"

"I can tolerate it. Actually no. I hate it. I wouldn't be able to get through this if my boyfriend weren't doing it with me. It would be hell. For us a romantic night is if we finish our homework before eleven get to watch Netflix for half an hour."

"How much longer till the CPA is done?"

"Don't remind me. Five, maybe six years."

I realized I shouldn't be so judgmental. Maybe all those shiny beautiful kids in Starbucks weren't guppies or Ken dolls, masturbating over their status. Maybe they were more like Lauren, busting their asses to achieve reasonably modest life milestones that were now considered dreams.

Before we parted, Lauren asked me for a favour. "Can we take a selfie?"

I hated taking photos. "Okay. Sure."

After she snapped a pic, she looked at me, dead serious. "Thank you, Tony. I need to show that I'm a well-rounded person who can socialize with colleagues. You know, for when potential employers do their social media checks."

"Are you using me to show that you're 'real?'"

"No … maybe." She smiled. "I do like to post pictures of friends too."

I laughed. "No problem. I get that. What filter are you going to use?"

"No filter. I'm trying to be real, remember?" She showed me the photo—I had made sure to angle my face so that my cheeks looked as chiselled as possible—and then walked into the Starbucks.

As I walked toward our usual table in Le Jardin, Lisa and Nick stood up to greet me. Lisa gave me air kisses and a hug. Nick, as always, put his fist out for me to bump, at which I'd look confused. He took his fist back and hugged me, saying the usual: "Sorry, I was with straight people earlier."

My entrance had interrupted Lisa telling a story.

"So he walks to me to my car. Asks if he can kiss me. I'm like, 'No.' What does he do? Grabs the sides of my face and pushes his face into mine. Gross dirty lips on my mouth."

"What the fuck? He grabbed your face and forced you to kiss him?" Nick asked.

"Yeah."

"What's his address? I'll fucking bust his face."

"That's sweet but calm yourself."

"What the fuck? Calm yourself?"

"Yeah. It's the new norm. You just get used to it."

"That's not normal. I'll kill him."

"Yeah, Lisa. It's not," I said.

"Okay guys, keep the testes in check. That's what caused the problem in the first place."

"Bullshit." Nick shook his head and rolled his eyes.

"So anyway. I just get in my car and drive away. Three days later I get this text. 'Sup?' Like, are you fucking kidding me?"

"What did you write back?"

"I haven't."

"Give me your phone," Nick said.

"No. I don't trust you. Tell me what to write."

"Just give me your phone."

"Can you just chill?"

"Fine. Write 'Thanks for the kiss the other night.'" Lisa typed as Nick continued. "'I have herpes btw.'"

We cackled like children.

Lisa typed it. "Sent! Thanks Nick."

We giggled again. "We're too old for this shit," Lisa said.

Nick's phone buzzed. He read the text message and looked upset.

"Everything okay?" I asked.

"Yeah, it's fine. How's work?"

"It's okay, I guess. I've been getting my shit in on time so that's good. I've been working a lot with Lauren, the intern. I always thought she was just this millennial—well, not the pretentious kind, you know? But holy shit, she's a work horse. Fucking robot. Doing CPA classes and volunteering too. I'm getting to like her. We're planning this this social work event in the next few weeks—bowling. She's bringing her boyfriend. Jell-O's bringing his wife."

"Oh really. You get to meet Mrs. Jell-O?"

"Yeah. And I'm bringing Antonio."

"What? Oh my God."

"Yeah. Lauren and Jell-O are excited to meet him. Jell-O told me he's so happy that I'm finally dating someone because apparently it's important to have a life outside of work. He's been so ... nice lately. Totally weird."

Just as the waiter came to take our order, Nick blurted out, "Lucas has been spending a lot of time with this guy from his yoga studio. I don't remember his name. I think he's the body flow instructor. He's having dinner with him tonight. Isn't that fucked up?"

The waiter pretended that someone was calling him and walked away.

"I thought you guys were open?" I asked.

"Well yeah. But he's had dinner with this guy twice now. Why do they have to go to dinner? They should just be doing it and that's all." Nick looked back down at his phone, shaking his head. He got up. "I gotta go to the bathroom."

The waiter came back. "Should I take your order or should I wait for him to come back?"

"No we know what we want," Lisa said. "I'll have the tuna. He'll have the house salad," gesturing to me.

"Actually no, not the salad," I said. "I'll have the banquet burger. With fries."

Lisa raised her eyebrows at me. "Oh. Good."

I didn't purge that burger up afterward, either. Nick, Lisa and I went to the Flamingo to catch a drink with Antonio after his shift. I wanted to throw up, though; I wasn't used to feeling full for a long period of time. In one session, Leslie had told us to use our willpower in the opposite way of dieters. "You have to will yourself to eat, because you have to eat in order to live," she said. It sounded so simple and logical.

Chapter 23: Gutter Balls

At first, Lauren had only been helping some of the other staff organize the first "Melo and Co. Social Event." But within a few weeks, she had completely taken over the whole thing, with me as her sidekick. She had planned it like a wedding; soon I found myself busy working on a project plan and running around town picking up name tags, decorations and even bonbonieres. Melo and Co. employed about a hundred people. All were invited. Thirty-five RSVP'd.

"Who's getting married?" Phil from IT asked, as Lauren and I carried in boxes of little goody bags.

"We're all getting married to the company," I said. "We're already prisoners, might as well celebrate it."

"So funny," Lauren said. "If we don't have fun, this is going to be a complete failure." She opened the door to Strikers, the bowling alley and dinner joint, letting us enter ahead of her.

A young hostess walked us to our area. They had set up three long dinner tables in the shape of a T.

"Okay, Tony, can you set up the go-away gifts, the prizes, and the guest lists? I'll start on the decorations. You and I can sit at the head table, greet everyone and check them off the list."

"Got it boss."

Lauren reached into one of the boxes. "Oh and don't forget to set out the place cards according to the seating plan."

"You made a seating plan?!" Phil asked.

"Of course," she said, "gotta make sure everyone feels like a special snowflake, right?"

Jell-O and his wife, Christine, were among the first to arrive, arguing while they walked toward the table. But as soon they locked eyes with Lauren and me, they were all big smiles. As if they had pushed their "on" buttons.

"Laur!" Jell-O pointed his index finger and pulled the trigger with his thumb. "This looks great! A lot more fun than the EFT account, eh?" he said, laughing as if it was the funniest thing ever. Christine rolled her eyes.

"Couldn't have done this without Tony," Lauren said, checking their names off the list.

Lauren's boyfriend, Kenny, arrived, looking concerned.

"What is it?" she asked.

"We did our entire presentation wrong—the Organizational Behavioural model for class. I was talking to Jenn, she said we took have to take a more strategic approach ... we have to align it to our mission statement, which needs to reflect to our vision statement, which has to support our objectives, which needs to reflect our tactics. We gotta redo the whole thing tonight if we're presenting tomorrow."

"What?" Lauren said. "But we already spent like five hours on it."

"I was thinking maybe we could just insert the word strategic everywhere in the PowerPoint and be done with it? All the words mean nothing anyway."

"I don't think it's that easy," Lauren huffed. "Oh God, I can't think about this right now. Kenny, go sit at the table. Mingle with my coworkers. Make sure you make our life sounds fabulous and important, okay?"

"All right."

The waitress was starting to take dinner orders and the chair beside me remained empty.

"Where's your friend?" Lauren asked.

"Not sure. Probably running late."

The waitress began rhyming off the specials of the day but stopped—nobody at the table was looking at her. Everybody had turned to look in my direction, at Antonio, who had just pecked me on the cheek and was taking off his jacket to sit down.

"Everyone, this is Antonio," I said. They all smiled politely. I looked back at the waitress: "Sorry, continue with the specials."

Lauren put her mouth to my hear. "Oh my God, Tony, you've got yourself a cutie."

I knew what everyone was thinking. *How* could he and I be together?

Soon the food came out. I watched a parade of beautiful dishes pass through my hands and down the table—three bacon cheeseburgers, chili nachos, seafood linguini, a bunch of mini pizzas—until my plate landed in front of its rightful owner.

Antonio looked at me with disapproval. "Salad. Again?"

"What? I don't want to overdo it."

He shook his head. "This is a party. You should enjoy yourself. I'll give you a bite of my chicken."

Lauren and Jell-O were giggling like children on the other side of me.

"What? Why are you two whispering and laughing?" I asked.

"Nothing," Jell-O said.

They stared at each other and chuckled.

"Okay, you can't do that. What is it? Come on."

"It's just ..." Jell-O paused. "It's so like ... cute... you and your boyfriend. You guys are so sweet together."

Did my boss just refer to me as cute? Sweet?

"Oh God please."

"No, don't get me wrong, Tones! Yes, I live in the burbs so I don't see a lot of ..."

"Of what?"

"You know, couples like you guys. But it's totally cool! Plus... I watch Modern Family, so I like know all about it." He gave me the thumbs up, leaned back in his chair and then took a sip of his beer. "I'm totally progressive," he said with a big smile.

Antonio leaned in. "What are you guys talking about?"

"Nothing."

Jell-O was more than buzzed. This could be an HR disaster. "I was just telling Tony about how I think you two are awesome together!"

"Ha-ha. Well, thanks."

Jell-O leaned in again. "So like ... which one of you ..."

Christine stopped him. "Victor, no! You've had too many beers."

"Oh, come on, Christine! This is my Tony-Tone! We're all bosom buddies here."

Lauren looked scared.

"So, uhhh ..." Jell-O nodded. "Which one of you is ... you know, the pitcher. And which one's the catcher?"

Christine placed her hand on his month. "I am absolutely mortified. Tony, do not answer that." She turned to Jell-O. "Honey, I cannot believe you. Tony, do not report him to HR, okay? I swear, every time he drinks Heineken, he gets like this."

"No, it's okay," Antonio said. "We're cool, we'll answer anything."

I turned to Antonio. "What are you doing?" I mumbled. He ignored me.

"See, honey," Jell-O said to Christine. "We're all cool here. These guys have no secrets from me! We all bros!" He laughed like a college frat boy.

Christine rolled her eyes. "Jesus."

Antonio leaned further in. "We really don't play baseball, you know? We're more like into fencing. We just like to jab each other. Right babe? Jab jab jab!" Antonio looked at me with a big smile. I looked away.

Everybody laughed.

"That's what I like to hear! Y'all jabbing each other!" Jell-O said, raising his glass for another drink. "I like you, Antonio! You're really cool." He turned to his wife. "I love this guy!"

"Oh, easy there, big guy, I'm taken," Antonio said.

The table erupted in laughter again.

"Okay okay, put that down and drink some water," Christine said, snatching the beer out of his hand. She looked at us. "I'm so sorry, guys. When Victor tries to act cool and relate to young people, this is what happens. Our teenage nieces and nephews are totally weirded out by him."

"It's okay," I said.

Lauren jumped in. "Actually it's nice just to interact with the team outside the office. And you know, not talk about quantifying and cutting."

Jell-O stuffed a bunch of nachos in his face and started talking as he chewed. "You know, Lauren, I'm so glad you said that. Because, you know what, we do spend a lot of time with each other. Do y'all hear me down there?" He shouted until all the tables looked at him. "I just wanted to say to everyone how happy I am that we can all get together and have some laughs outside the office."

Everybody smirked or giggled and then went back to their conversations.

"Oh fuck it, I lost 'em. Whatever." Jell-O took another drink of his beer, which he'd grabbed back from Christine. "You know guys, as I was saying but was so rudely ignored, we spend a lot of time with each other. Hell, I see you guys more than I see my family. So we might as well be friends, right?"

Lauren nodded.

Jell-O continued. "Ever since we rolled out those new initiatives, I really feel a change in our environment."

"What initiatives?" Antonio asked.

"You know, encouraging the work-life balance, team-building events, letting people work from home … eventually there'll be some daily stretch breaks and improvements in our benefits," Jell-O said.

"It's the least you can do, after making our office look like a laboratory," Phil said. "Oh sorry Victor, just trying to be honest."

"It's fine. I know," Jell-O said. "But I'm just happy that we're doing some things to try to make the staff like the company they work for. You guys aren't just robots, you know? Good people are scarce, and these millennials keep jumping … we need to retain the good ones."

"That's great to hear," I said.

"And that's just the start of it, Tony-Tones! Eventually we'll have a better employee assistance plan. Maybe access to a dietician."

Christine interrupted. "Yeah, maybe he can finally get rid of this baby," she said, rubbing Jell-O's stomach.

Suddenly a feeling came over me. What a cruel thing for a spouse to say.

"Ha-ha, funny, honey," Jell-O said to her. He then turned to me and Lauren. "You know, I've gotta get my diabetes under control."

Lauren looked down at her itinerary. "Oh my goodness, guys, we're behind schedule. We need to start bowling now!"

"But Tony-Tones hasn't even eaten his salad," Jell-O said.

Every looked at me and my half-eaten bowl of Caesar salad.

"It's okay, I'm not that hungry."

Lauren had divided us into teams. Antonio and I were with Phil and his girlfriend, and Julie from sales. Lauren and her boyfriend were with Jell-O, Christine and a woman from accounting I didn't know. Her name was Wendy.

I scanned the florescent-coloured balls on the racks. I hadn't been bowling in years. I reached for a bright yellow thirteen-pounder, but it was too heavy, even if I used both hands.

"Come on, babe, use those guns!" Antonio said as he squeezed my biceps. "Jesus, your arms ... never mind." He reached down and picked a ball for himself. "I think I need a fourteen-pounder."

"Fourteen-pounder? If I can't pick up thirteen pounds, there's no way you can handle fourteen."

Antonio hefted the ball in front of his face. "Sure I can. Like it?" he asked. It was florescent pink with silver sparkles.

"Shines just like you, honey," I said.

I looked around further but found myself unable to lift a twelve, eleven, or even ten-pound ball. "What's the lightest ball you have?" I asked a staff member.

"Nine pounds. I think there's a few near the kids' lanes."

"Thanks."

I gathered up all my strength and was able to lift one up using both hands.

Lauren was a surprisingly excellent bowler. She even had the knee bend and pivot when she threw. Kenny later told me she had bowled competitively as a kid, and would throw fits if she didn't win.

"So now we know why Lauren wanted bowling for this event, eh?" Jell-O hollered.

"It's either win or nothing, Victor. If we lose, someone will just have to die!" I'd never seen her as intense about something other than work.

Antonio went up and bowled a strike, of course. Perfect little shit.

"What are you doing?" I said to him aside. "I'm supposed to be the star here. You're just supposed to look good beside me!"

"Oh, honey. You want me to be a trophy wife! So sweet!" he said back, loud enough for everyone to hear. "But I can't help it if I'm fabulous, okay?"

"You guys are adorable!" Jell-O called. "I love you guys."

"And I love straight people!" Antonio yelled back.

Everybody laughed. Antonio turned to me. "See honey, the straights love me!"

It was my turn to bowl. "Come on, Tony!" yelled Phil. I walked over to pick up my ball, but it still felt too heavy. *Dammit, I'm too weak.* I should have eaten the whole salad.

"You need help there, honey?" Antonio said walking up beside me.

"No, I got it."

I reached down with both hands and managed to get it off the rail. I walked toward to the top of the lane. This should be easy, I thought. Just take one hand off, and roll it down the middle. But when I took my left hand off, the ball was too heavy for my right hand and it dropped. I saw it fall in slow motion, but all of a sudden I was hopping on my left leg. "Oh shit!" I screamed in pain.

I didn't think it was broken, but the nail on my big toe turned dark red, then purple within ten minutes.

I bowled with two hands for the rest of the night.

An hour and a half and many shots and beers later, we had bowled two games. Jell-O and Lauren's team won the first, and my team won the second. Surprisingly, I wasn't doing too badly with my double-handed bowling method. I managed to get two spares, and I never hit fewer than seven pins in every round. I'm pretty sure it was the adrenaline that kept me going, because I was running low on energy, and the ball was getting unbearably heavy.

We were nearing the end of the third game and Lauren's and my team were tied. It all came down to the last frame, and the last two bowlers were Lauren and me. By that point, Jell-O was so inebriated that he had sat the last two frames out.

"You got this," Kenny said, trying to psych Lauren up.

"I got this," she said. She turned around and threw the ball in her perfect stance, pivot and knee bend. But the ball slowly drifted to the left and only knocked down five pins. "Shit!" she yelled.

"It's okay, babe."

Lauren picked up the ball for her second throw. Again, the ball drifted off to the side, this time into the gutter. She turned around, shoulders slumped, and consoled herself in Kenny's arms. The rest of her team tried to cheer her up, with no success.

"Good job," Jell-O mumbled.

"Okay, Tony! All you have to hit is six pins, and we win!" Phil said. "First prize is a free dinner at that fancy place on Yonge ... what's it called? I forget, but I know a couple of caviar eggs are like fifty bucks."

"Thanks, Phil. That sounds pretty fancy."

I picked up my ball with both hands and walked toward the lane.

I heard Antonio's voice: "Baby, if you win this, you get to be the pitcher tonight!"

Everybody laughed. I turned around in disbelief. Antonio smiled as if to say "don't worry, they love me!"

"Dude, I love this guy!" Jell-O said, taking another swig of his beer. I rolled my eyes. Lauren was still in Kenny's arms, looking upset.

"Don't worry babe," I heard him say to her. "They won't think less of you because of a gutter ball. Forget it. Besides we gotta redo that entire presentation tonight, remember? Right now *is* the highlight of the evening."

"Oh great," Lauren said sarcastically.

I turned around and looked at the pins at the end of the lane. *Six pins.*

I rolled the ball into the right gutter.

"It's okay, hon. You've got another shot," Antonio said.

I rolled the second ball into the left gutter.

Lauren's team looked at each other in disbelief and started jumping up and down. "Woo-hoo! We're eating caviar!" Jell-O yelled.

Phil came over and patted my back. "Good try, bud."

The excitement on Lauren's face when her team won was worth it.

***

Exercise 5.0: Mindfulness

Mindfulness is the awareness that emerges through paying attention on purpose, in the present moment and non-judgmentally to things as they are. Pay attention to what? you might ask. To anything, but especially to those aspects of life that that we most take for granted or ignore. For instance, we might start paying attention to the basic components of experience, like how we feel, what is on our minds, and how we perceive or know anything at all. Mindfulness means paying attention to things as they actually are in any given moment, however they are, rather than as we want them to be. Why does paying attention in this way help? Because it is the exact antithesis to the type of ruminative thinking that makes low moods persist and return.

Eating One Raisin: A First Taste of Mindfulness
1. Holding
    a. First, take a raisin and hold it in the palm of your hand or between your finger and thumb.

b. Focusing on it, imagine that you've just dropped in from Mars and have never seen an object like this before in your life.

2. Seeing

a. Take time to really see it; gaze at the raisin with care and full attention.

b. Let your eyes explore every part of it, examining the highlights where the light shines, the darker hollows, the folds and ridges, and any asymmetries or unique features.

3. Touching

a. Turn the raisin over between your fingers, exploring its texture, maybe with your eyes closed if that enhances your sense of touch.

4. Smelling

a. Holding the raisin between your nose, with each inhalation drink in any smell, aroma, or fragrance that may arise, noticing as you do this anything interesting that may be happening in your mouth or stomach.

5. Placing

a. Now slowing bring the raisin up to your lips, noticing how your hand and arm know exactly how and where to position it. Gently place the object in the mouth, without chewing, noticing how it gets into the mouth in the first place. Spend a few moments exploring the sensations of having it in your mouth, exploring it with your tongue.

6. Tasting

a. When you are ready, prepare to chew the raisin, noticing how and where it needs to be for chewing. Then, very consciously, take one or two bites into it and notice what happens in the aftermath, experiencing any waves of taste that emanate from it as you continue chewing. Without swallowing yet, notice the bare sensations of taste and texture in the mouth and how these may change over time, moment by moment, as well as any changes in the object itself.

7. Swallowing
    a. When you feel ready to swallow the raisin, see if you can first detect the intention to swallow as it comes up, so that even this is experienced consciously before you actually swallow the raisin.

8. Following
    a. Finally, see if you can feel what is left of the raisin moving down into your stomach, and sense how the body as a whole is feeling after completing this exercise in mindful eating.

I got to group 15 minutes early, hoping to take a nap on the big couch before the session. But I walked into the room to find April already there.

"Oh. Hi."

"Hi," she said, without looking up from her phone.

I sat on the opposite couch. "I'm just going to shut my eyes for a bit." She still didn't look up.

I put my head on the arm of the couch and used my jacket as a blanket, shutting my eyes. I heard April shifting around in her seat, and then footsteps coming closer. Suddenly there was a plop on my couch. I opened my eyes to a huge mop of curly hair beside me. April's eyes zoomed into my face.

"Tony, right?"

"Yeah."

"What did you think of the last material? It's fucking bullshit, right? So useless."

I looked around to make sure nobody could hear us. "Yeah, I tried it but felt stupid."

"I know, right? Sometimes the shit we do here is so dumb."

She reached into her bag and pulled out some wrapped Hershey chocolate. "Wanna kiss?" she said.

"Should you be bringing that here?"

"Oh whatever. Nobody's around."

She gave me a few and we ate as she continued talking.

"Hershey kisses are my drug," she said.

I chuckled.

"You don't talk much in group. You're bulimic, right? That's what you said?"

"Um... *what*?"

"But you look like you could be a starver too."

"You mean I look like I'm anorexic?"

"Yeah." She looked down at my hand. "Wait, you've got bite marks on your knuckles." I crossed my arms to cover them.

"I purge too." She seemed delighted in this commonality. "Tell me. What do you do?"

"What do you mean?"

"You know, what are your tricks?"

"Tricks for what?"

"Your tricks or tips for getting it out of you?

"Oh."

"Yeah. Like a list or rules you go by."

How did she know I had rules?

"I guess I kind of have a list in my head."

"Oh good. Me too. So spill! What do you use? All I need is one finger."

I looked around again and listened for footsteps coming down the hall.

"Oh my God."

"Come on."

"I need two fingers. One is too skinny."

"What are you trying to do, one-up me?"

"One-up you?"

"Yeah, let's not play that game, Tony. We're too old for this."

"You're a kid. What are you … sixteen?"

"Nineteen. So what else?"

"No. I *cannot* believe we are doing this."

"Oh, whatever. It's fun. Chopsticks?"

"That's racist. And no."

"Straws."

"Straws?"

"Yup."

"Toothbrush."

"Me too. Laxatives? "

"Ex-lax chocolates. Mmm."

"Sienna stool softener."

"Diuretics."

"Meal replacement? I like coffee."

"Me too, with skim milk. Gum."

"Green tea."

"Crackers."

"Too many carbs."

"Are you judging me?"

"I'm not judging. Anyway … cucumbers."

"Vegetable broth."

"I'd get bloated. I sit in saunas—gets rid of all water retention—your bones look sharp after."

"That's a good tip, April."

"Thanks."

I couldn't believe we were talking about this. A few seconds of silence passed.

"April?"

"Yeah?"

"You ever heard about this inpatient program at St. Paul's? It's like three months long."

"Yeah. I heard you *have* to eat there."

"That's what my shrink said."

"Fuck that," she said. "I'd rather kill myself than go there. I'd swallow staples or paperclips or something to get transferred out … I'd find a way to escape."

About ten minutes later, Leslie walked in with her clipboard. She quickly took attendance. Our group had dwindled from twelve on week one to eight regular attendees.

"Okay, how did we all feel about the mindfulness exercise?" Leslie asked the group.

"You mean the raisin thing?" Amanda asked.

"Yeah. What was it like for you Amanda?"

"Umm. It was interesting."

"How so?"

"I never took that much time to eat something, especially something that small."

"Is that true for everyone?" Leslie asked the group. We all nodded. "I'm going to go around the room now and ask each of you what you learned from the exercise. Amanda, continue."

"Well I learned that I really don't take much time to think about eating when I'm eating."

"Okay, great."

Leslie turned to Shelley.

"I learned that raisins are a lot more flavourful than I thought."

We continued around the circle, everyone giving similar responses:

"It was interesting."

"Um, yeah, interesting."

"That's interesting," Leslie said after each one.

She was interested by them being interested. You had to hand it to her—through repeated, generic, and one-word responses from the group, she always kept a straight face. Meanwhile, I was surprised April hadn't managed to roll her eyes out of her head every time somebody claimed to think something was "interesting."

Finally, after a few non-descript answers, Leslie cut to the chase. "Okay guys, I think the important thing here is that we found ourselves actively trying to be present in the moment. To just eat the raisin and notice the experience as it is, and not judge it. If you apply this to other activities that don't involve eating, it really helps in your everyday life. If you experience each moment as it is, rather than painting that moment with a thought or judgment of your own, it can really help you get control of your eating disorder.

Leslie noticed April looking at her cynically.

"April," Leslie said with caution. "What do you think about the raisin exercise?"

"Well, the raisin didn't start a binge," she quipped.

A few group members smirked, while others focused on Leslie's reaction.

"Okay April, that's not funny."

"Honestly? Can I just say it?"

"Of course, April. This is a safe place."

"I think it's bullshit."

Leslie paused. "What is? The exercise or the ideas or—"

"Everything," April interrupted. "Being in the present sounds lovely and straight out of a warm and fuzzy intervention book. But how does that help us not to binge and purge? I don't get it."

Many of the group members seemed to agree in silence. April had said it out loud for all of us.

"I don't mean to be a difficult, Leslie. But all these exercises, all these beautiful and poetic pearls of wisdom you give us, and all these activities we do … it's all bullshit. They seem to be revelations, but they're totally not practical. We can't apply most of these to our everyday lives. All inspirational mantras … meaningless."

"They're not meaningless. You can apply all of them," Leslie said.

"No, you can't."

"Yes, actually you can."

"You don't understand, Leslie."

"That's okay, just help me understand."

This seemed to infuriate April. "Like, what am I supposed to do when I'm depressed because I find out I'm failing math, or when my parents are fighting downstairs, or when my dad throws my scale at me and yells, "eat for fucks sake!" What am I supposed to do? Be present? Be aware? Okay. I'm *aware* that there's a scale being thrown at my head and I'm *aware* my dad is yelling at me. Can't stop me from crying. But hey, you know what, I'm present, I'm aware… that must mean everything is fine! Fucking win!" Her voice got shaky. "I'm sorry. I should go."

She grabbed her bag and jacket and ran out of the room without making eye contact with anyone. Leslie followed, calling to her from the entrance. "April, come back. April. It's okay, come back."

Leslie came back to the room a few minutes later with wet puffy eyes. Her voice was thin and frail for the rest of the session. She tried to hide how upset she was by nodding and smiling more often than usual.

I had an appointment with Dr. Tee the next Tuesday.

"Wow," Dr. Tee said. "That sounds intense."

"It was. I'd be surprised if she came back."

"What do you think, Tony? Was she right?"

"Yeah. I think so. All this advice and stuff seems like common sense, but really you can't keep up with all that every day. I can't keep up with a food journal every day. I can't do most of it. It's exhausting. I just want to be normal."

"Normal is different for everyone, Tony. The idea that there's only one kind of normal for everyone is an illusion."

"Oh God, now you sound like the group. Cliché after cliché."

"Fair enough."

"So, this mindfulness—they want us to focus on the moment as it is, right? And not to judge it?"

"Yeah, that's right."

"What about those times when the moment, as it is, just sucks, without you having to judge it? April was right. Like she said, when her parents are yelling at her or throwing shit at her? Or if I make a mistake at work? There's no judging needed—those times suck, objectively or subjectively or whatever."

Dr. Tee looked at me in silence.

I continued. "Are your parents still alive?"

"My mom is. My dad passed about five years ago."

"That was sad, right?"

"Of course."

"That's what I'm saying. When my mom died, I was ..." I stopped. Better not to get into it to avoid an ugly cry.

I went back to talking about the session: "Mindfulness says not to judge those moments where we experience turmoil, but just be aware of them? How can you be aware of moments like those without feeling like you want to jump off a bridge?"

"Well, I think—"

I cut him off. "Really then, the way to not get depressed is to *not* feel sadness. To *not* think about how bad the situation is. That makes sense doesn't it? The reason happy people are happy is because they don't think too much. They're fucking stupid. Or they just don't feel sad emotions. They're robots… I want to be robot, Dr. Tee."

Dr. Tee was hastily scribbling on his notepad.

"And another thing," I continued, "how are you supposed to figure out your self-worth according to a pie chart?"

"Okay, I understand what you're saying, Tony." He shook his head and leaned back in his chair. He sighed. "Let's weigh you just to see where you're at."

"Sorry. Fine."

I took off my shoes and jacket. "Should I take off my hoodie too?" I always asked if I could take all my clothes off to get the lowest number possible.

"No, that's fine."

I stepped on the scale—98 pounds.

Fuck. I've gained.

"Isn't that good?" I asked, smirking. "I'm over ninety-five."

"You're still under your ideal BMI, Tony."

Chapter 25: Monologue A

After my session with Dr. Tee, I felt adventurous. I decided to try portion control. I opened the freezer, took a carton of ice cream out and shoved a spoon in.

Just one bite. That's it. When you're done, you're going to put it back in the freezer. Maybe tomorrow, you can have another spoonful.

I put the spoon in my mouth—morgasm.

I was interrupted by the doorbell. It was Antonio.

"Tony! Holy shit! Holy shit!" he said excitedly.

"What happened? Why didn't you text me first?" I asked.

He walked in immediately, grabbed the carton and spoon out of my hand, and shoved the scoop of ice cream into his face. He launched into a monologue, talking much faster than usual.

"So I walk by the bathroom and see my little sister doing her hair. And it's a mess. Bitch looks like a Shakira nightmare, okay? So I ask her, 'What is up with your hair?' and Kim's like, 'What do you mean?' and I'm like, 'You look like a Shakira nightmare,' and she's like, 'Shut up. I teased it. Steve's bringing me to meet his mother. I can't not tease it,' and I can't help it and I'm like, 'Bitch, gimme the straight iron.' So I start fixing that shit up. Then Kim's like, 'Why are you home? Shouldn't you be out with your friend Tony?' and I'm like, 'Uh yeah. I wanted to tell you.' And she's like, 'Where's my eyelash curler? Antonio, did you take it again?' and I'm like, 'No it's right on the counter.' So she's trying to do her eyelashes and she's fumbling with the curler and shit and I'm like, 'Oh my God, give it to me,' so I snatch it out of her hand and work on her eyes. And she's like, 'Oh my God, oow that hurts,' and I'm like, 'Honey please, beauty is pain.' So then I'm like, 'Yeah, so my friend Tony. We're kind of...' and then I froze. Kim's like, 'I know.' And I'm like, 'You know?' And she's like, 'Yeah I know,' and I'm like, 'How do you know? Wait, what do you know?' She's like, 'That you and Tony are together!' and I'm like, 'Oh my God, you know!' And then I'm like, 'So, is that okay?' and she's like, 'What difference does it make?' and I'm like, 'No, I mean are you okay with it?' and she's like, 'Yeah, why not?' So I was like, 'Oh, okay great.' And she's like, 'I don't think anything weirds me out anymore. Except if you told me you were doing like the transgender thing. Then I'd be like ... um ... well actually, I think it would be really cool 'cuz then we could trade clothes and shit. But then you're skinnier than me. I fucking hate you Tono.' I didn't know what to say next, I was so relieved, right? And then Kim's like, 'Okay, I just have one question,' and I'm like, 'What?' and she's like, 'Do you think Tony's bigger than Steve?' and I'm like, 'What? Eww!' and she's like, 'There's no way anyone is bigger than Steve—you know what they say about brown guys,' and I'm like, 'Eww I'm not having this conversation with you.' And then she's like, 'Wait, I have pictures on my phone, hold on,' and she runs to get the phone and I'm like, 'Fuck off, there's no way I'm looking at that.'"

Antonio took another heaping scoop of ice cream.

"Tony darling!" his eyes widened. "This is huge! I finally came out to her. I didn't think it would be so easy! Maybe I can get her to slip it to my mom, and then I wouldn't have to come out to her. She'd know and could process it and not have that initial freak-out reaction on me! You know, the passive aggressive indirect thing or whatever. That would be awesome. I'm think that's how I'll tell my mom. How's your day?"

Antonio's optimism stirred something in me. How could I look at things with the same rose coloured—no actually hot pink—glasses as he did?

I could have used the hot pink glasses later that week.

Another secret truth I've figured out is how someone can get themselves depressed in the most efficient manner: browse LinkedIn.

On my way home from the Light House on Thursday night, I got a random connection request from Sean Langston, a kid I went to elementary and high school with. I hadn't seen him in fifteen years, not since *the incident*. When we were eight, we used to chase each other with water guns and play tag at recess. Years later when we entered high school, he first acted as if he didn't know me. Then by second semester, he had started yelling "faggot" at me in the cafeteria, along with the other boys from the football team. Even though I was hurting on the inside, I still thought he was cute.

Sean's LinkedIn picture was unrecognizable. He had lost most of his golden wavy hair, and his chubby cheeks were anchored by a double, maybe even triple chin. Was this the same guy? I wanted to pat myself on the back; despite my many issues, I looked better now than I had as a teenager.

But here was the kicker: Sean was a partner at Deloitte, and had his CPA. Sean Langston, the kid who couldn't understand fractions in grade three, who was in the lowest academic stream in high school at least till grade ten, had gotten into McMaster for commerce, and according to the awards section on his LinkedIn profile, made the Dean's List?

But I had to remind myself: life doesn't make sense. Just because he was a tool who happened to be a monster in high school didn't mean he didn't deserve a good life. Maybe he had changed.

"What are you looking at?" Antonio asked.

"Just looking at this request I got on LinkedIn. I can't believe he's a fucking CPA and partner at Deloitte."

"De-what?" Antonio asked.

"Deloitte. It's a big consulting firm. I don't get it."

"What?"

"He must be making a shitload of money. But he was a fucking idiot in school."

"You gotta stop doing that, babe," Antonio said.

"What?"

"Comparing yourself to others. It's always going to be bad."

"Fine."

"That shit on social media is all fake anyway. He's probably a janitor."

"No, he's not. You could get fired if you lied online," I said.

"Okay. Well, whether he's a partner or a janitor, does it make a difference to your life?"

"No."

"You're welcome," he said.

Something triggered me. "You know what, you can't just walk around thinking you know everything, okay?"

"Okay, what are you talking about now?"

"You don't know what happened with this guy, so you can't just blurt shit out like you're Dr. Phil."

Antonio's voice intensified. "Okay, you know what, I'm getting sick of you being all cynical and shit."

"I'm not cynical. I'm just realistic."

"You're so negative."

"What? Am I hurting your chakra? You stupid entitled kids."

"He's a partner, good for him. Let it go. You're too worked up all the time."

"I can't just let it go, okay. It's not that easy."

"Why not?"

"Okay, Antonio, let me tell you a little about Sean from LinkedIn," I said, my voice raised.

"Go ahead," Antonio said. "School me once again, old wise master."

I thought of all the things I wanted to spew out at him. I thought about how good it would feel to put him in his place. The monologue sounded like a beautiful raging symphony in my head:

Fine, smartass. So I grew up with Sean, right? We were friends in grade school. Then it changed when we got older. Instead of calling me by my name, he called me "faggot" along with everyone else. "Hey faggot! How's it going, faggot? Why you looking at me, faggot?" One day in grade 11 gym class, we're playing basketball, right? As usual, nobody passes me the ball. It's the final seconds of the game, we're behind by two points and there's nobody open to throw a three pointer, except me. Sean passes to me and yells, "Take the shot faggot, win this for us." I miss... the ball doesn't touch the rim. When the class ends, I run to the change room so I can get out as soon as I can. As I'm taking a shower, I hear, "You lost the game for us, faggot." I turn around and see Sean and maybe four other boys standing in front of me with their dicks out their shorts. So I walk toward the exit but Sean stops me. "Where you going, faggot? Isn't this what you want? A fucking gang bang?" I tell him to fuck off, and he pushes me. "What the fuck did you say to me?" I fall back and my shoulder slams into the shower wall. "Hold him down!" Sean's yelling. Two of 'em tackle me to the ground and have me face-down, staring into the drain. One pins my arms behind me and the other sits on my legs. Sean keeps saying, "This is what you want, faggot!

Hurry up, let's do it, guys!" I scream for help but another kid covers my mouth with his hand and tells me to "shut the fuck up, faggot pussy." I feel the shower on my back ... then I see the stream leading to the drain turn yellow.

I shut my eyes so the piss wouldn't get in them, and just waited till it was over. When I went home, I cried, but couldn't tell my mother why. I was too ashamed. When the principal found out, Sean and the other four boys were suspended for a week. We didn't talk or make eye contact for the rest of high school. That was the big juicy gossip that students and teachers would whisper to each other about me but never said out loud. I was the faggot that the boys pissed on.

It would have been amazing to let that all out. But I didn't say it. I always thought of that platitude, "if you don't have something nice to say, then don't say anything at all."

So I held it all in, like I had in the past.

Swallow the hurt, swallow the resentment. Hold in as much pain you can. Vomit out everything else.

9:15 a.m. on Friday. Time to meet with Jell-O and the HR rep for my daily Performance Improvement Plan check-in.

There were a couple of different HR reps. They'd rotate. Mondays and Thursdays we'd meet with Karen. Then Tuesdays, Wednesdays and Fridays would be Khalid. Jell-O did most of the talking in these meetings while the rep would sit and check things off a spreadsheet.

"Tony, when's the last time you filled out an incident report?" Jell-O asked me.

"Not since we started this Performance Improvement Plan," I said.

"Yeah, I thought so. That's good. So you've been getting everything in on time."

"Yeah, I guess so."

Karen checked off a couple of boxes on her spreadsheet.

Jell-O shuffled through some papers in my file. "I reviewed your work on the Cisco project yesterday. It was really well done, Tony."

"Thanks."

"Lauren also told me you've been a great help on the EFT account."

"Oh good. Yeah, I like working with her."

"Great."

Jell-O closed the file and looked at me. "I'm definitely pleased to see things looking up. You did a great job on the audit, and our bowling event, too."

I nodded.

Jell-O continued, smiling. "Tony-Tone, say what. I'm gonna put you back on the EFT account as the lead. How do you feel about that?"

"Yeah, sure. Looking forward to it."

"Great. We'll see how it goes and then from there, maybe we'll talk about you not assisting Lauren anymore. Do your own work. And then take you off of this improvement plan? How does that sound, big guy?" Jell-O said.

"Really?" I asked.

"Yes sir-ee." He looked at Karen. "Karen, are we all on the same page here?"

"Definitely, Victor," Karen said. She loved Jell-O's catch phrases. Office people loved catch phrases. And acronyms. Jargon. "Great, I've added this to the file. Let's aim for next week. Then we can call these sessions done like dinner."

I nodded and smiled as she walked out the door.

"Tony. I'm so glad you're back. You had me worried for a while there, boss." He chuckled.

"Thanks."

I noticed that as my work performance improved, Jell-O had begun to make small talk with me again. It was a bit of a relief; a warning sign that you were getting fired was the big wigs not initiating small talk with you.

As we walked out of the room he turned to me. "I know it's your birthday soon, big guy. You doing anything special?"

"Not much," I said. "Just dinner with friends."

"Antonio too, right? I love that guy!" He opened the door for me. "Great work again, Tony."

Work was not the only thing that was looking up. For the last few weeks, I had not had one binge or purge episode. That was the longest span I had gone without any vomiting episodes. Between focusing on my work, doing the CBT exercises at the Light House, (even though I was still critical of some of them) and hanging with Antonio, I had been too distracted to think about it.

After work I went to the grocery store. There's one area that taunts me whenever I pass: the bulk food section. Where you have the freedom to choose exactly the volume of food you want within the restrictions of a plastic bag.

Earlier in my eating disorder, I thought the bulk food section was a great way to eat whatever I wanted in a controlled portion. I could have one scoop of chocolate almonds, that was it, as opposed to a whole bag-full if I bought it off the shelf. That's why I could never keep large volumes of food in the house—be it cereal boxes, bags of chips, or containers of ice cream—because if I had one taste, I'd lose control and have to finish the entire thing. All or nothing. I read a study that people who diet or fast are most susceptible to binges because when their bodies get a hint of food, their senses become activated and immediately demand more. Deprivation leads to over indulgence. This was certainly true for me. Every time I ate, it was like my taste buds rose from the dead, screaming. They could only be silenced by smothering them with food.

As I slowly got more restrictive with my calories, I stopped using the bags for little "harmless" portions, and instead began snatching single samples from the bins, shoving them right into my mouth and hurrying away.

Thief.

Many times, this is what I called dinner for the night. I'd walk into the grocery store, swipe one of something, and walk right out. *I only want one,* I told myself. *I only need one...* It was stupid to put one or two pieces in the bag, only to have to try to avoid eye contact with the cashier when paying for it, I reasoned. Plus, how are customers to know if they like how something tastes unless they try it? This was how I rationalized what I was doing.

I hadn't done it in a while, and I saw a bin of broken Oh Henry pieces. I looked around to make sure there was no staff nearby, walked toward the bin, snatched a couple of pieces, stuffed one in my face and turned around quickly.

It tasted amazing. Morgasm.

As I walked away, I heard a familiar voice.

"Excuse me, sir." I turned around. It was a store clerk, her messy grey hair coming out of her hat. She was that sweet grandmother type.

"You can't just sample from the bins. You have to put it in a bag and buy like everyone else."

"Oh, I'm sorry," I said. "I was just sampling. How much do I owe you, or should I pay at the front?"

"That's okay, dear. Just remember for next time."

"I will. Thank you."

I rushed out of the store, relieved; she had given me that same warning two times before—maybe last year—but didn't remember me.

I sat in my car and excitedly reached into my pocket—another piece of chocolate from the bin. I wolfed it down and felt my saliva running up my throat. And validating the study, I felt I needed more. I wanted to binge. I compiled a case for a binge, coming up with the following justifications: 1. I haven't enjoyed myself in so long and have been disciplined for a while. 2. I had a good day at work—I'm almost off the PIP. And 3. It's my birthday soon—so I deserve a treat.

Variables weighed, decision reached.

I drove to one of my favourite plazas—it had a pizza joint, a burger joint, and an ice cream store. A one stop shop. I felt like starting with pizza today; within ten minutes, I had eaten two slices. With a Diet Coke. You always need something fizzy.

Next came the burger and fries. Out of the pizza place and into the burger joint next door, making sure the pizza staff didn't see me entering for another gorge. But what if they did? I could be picking food up for someone else, right?

After finishing the fries, my pressure of my belly against my belt indicated it was time for dessert. So I went to the ice cream shop for a two-scoop sundae. I was completely stuffed after the first scoop, but I would never *not* finish the rest. Not just with ice cream, but with everything. Even if the food didn't taste good anymore, I would just keep going.

I drove home quickly to my toilet to undo everything from the last half-hour. About ten minutes after starting to purge, I was interrupted by loud banging at the front door. I had only thrown up twice, so I was far from finished. But the banging got louder.

Eventually, I heard Antonio shouting through the door: "Babe! I know you're in there. Your car's in the driveway. Babe? Hello? Knock knock!"

Shit. What the hell is he doing here? We weren't supposed to see each other until the next day for my birthday.

"Babe. I'm not leaving until you open the door," he said, continuing to knock. My phone started ringing. He wasn't going away.

"Hello?"

"Tony, what the eff? Open the door. Everything okay?"

"Yeah, but can you come back later. I'm not feeling well."

"What? No. Are you okay? Open the door."

"Okay fine. Just gimme a minute."

I flushed the toilet and splashed cold water on my face. Tried to rid smell of vomit in my mouth. I ran down the hall and opened the door. He stood there holding a single red rose.

"Happy birthday!" He jumped up and hugged me. "Oh my God,

you okay? Have you been crying?" he asked.

"No, I'm fine. Just something in my eye."

"Okay. Well, I have a surprise for your birthday!"

"It's not till tomorrow." He handed me the rose. "Thank you. It's beautiful."

"Wanna know where I got it from?"

"Where?"

He reached out. "Give me your hand. I want to show you something. But you have to close your eyes," he said. He was like a giddy child.

"What? Antonio, I just got home from work. Let me change and—"

"Hush darling!" He took my hand, pulled me close and covered my eyes with his other hand. "Let's go."

"Where are we going? Let me get my keys."

"No, it's not far."

He led me outside my front door a few steps down and around the side of the house. I could hear the backyard gate to my open.

"Almost there," he said.

"Okay. Can I open my eyes now?"

"Hold on."

We walked a few more steps.

"Ready?" he asked.

"Yeah."

"Okay."

He removed his hand from my eyes. We were in my backyard, but I barely recognized it. The grass had been cut and the weeds removed. In the centre of the lawn and along the sides were newly planted rose bushes. They had already bloomed—bright reds and dark pinks, like the ones in Antonio's painting, and more piercing than any filter on Instagram.

A picture of my mom's garden flashed in my mind.

Had I gone back in time?

"What the—?" I said. I looked around in circles. "It's amazing. It's beautiful. How did you … when … holy shit."

"Yo mamma's not the only one with a green thumb, my darling," he said with a big smile.

"When? Wait, how did you even get back here?"

"Um honey, did you know that basically anyone can access your backyard? Why don't you have a lock on it? Little Portugal can be ghetto!"

"I didn't think I needed one. I figured that since I had killed everything back here, nobody would even want to come in."

"You've been working so late all the time. So I'd come before my class, do a little bit here and there. I can't believe you didn't notice anything. I was waiting for you to say something, and I was like, "why ain't dis bitch look out the window to see this miracle I'm performing in his own damn yard?"

"Sorry. Sometimes after work I just come home and go straight to bed. I guess I avoid looking back there. I killed it and then forgot about it."

"Well, I've resurrected it! It is dead no more, honey. No more of these nightmares of your mom telling you that you killed her flowers and shit!"

"Antonio. I can't believe you did this. This is the best present—" My eyes welled up.

Antonio's voice suddenly sounded serious: "Flowers are God's way of showing us all the pretty things that life can be. You deserve all the pretty roses that life has to offer, Tony. You deserve them all."

"What'd you say?"

"You deserve all the pretty roses that life has to offer. It's true."

Déjà vu. What he said, the place he stood. Déjà vu.

He took a step closer, put his hands to sides of my face and kissed me. Like in a movie. Rachmaninoff's Piano Concerto no. 2 played in my head. I moved my face closer to his neck, trying to get high off the smell of cake.

He stopped and took a step back.

"Eww, why do you taste like that? Like puke or something. Did you throw up?" he asked.

"No..."

He glared at me.

"Well, yeah," I mumbled.

"What? You sick?"

"No."

I didn't know what to say. I looked away.

Antonio's face changed again. He turned around and rushed back into the house.

Shit.

I followed, walking to the end of the hall, into the bathroom. He was standing there, staring down at the vomit floating in the toilet.

"I knew it," he said.

Fuck, it didn't flush all away. I'd been in such a rush to answer the door I didn't notice.

"It all makes sense now. I knew it," he said again.

"I just ate something bad. I was feeling sick. So I had to get rid of it."

"Tony ... ?" His voice was noticeably lower.

"What?"

"Do you think I'm stupid?"

I knew what he was saying. But I hoped he wouldn't say it.

He did.

"You don't think I notice? How anxious you get whenever you eat? You think I can't see when you look in a mirror? I knew there was something!"

"I know, okay. I'm working on it. I'm seeing a doctor. And I'm in a support group. I'm getting there," I said.

"But why? You look great as you are."

"I look like this *because* of this."

He shook his head.

"I don't know. I'm messed up, okay," I said.

"Why didn't you tell me?"

"Cause I feel like an idiot."

"What?"

"I'm supposed to have my shit together. I'm older than you. But I don't have anything together. This quarter-life crisis won't go away."

He came over and put his hands on my shoulders. He rested his chin on the top of my head, moving his hands up and down my back.

"I was going to tell you," I said. "I'm sorry. It's okay if this is all too much for you."

"Don't say sorry. We're going to fix this."

"We?"

"Yeah."

"That's nice of you to say. But I'm not going to put this on you."

"Shut up, Tony."

I told him all about my eating disorder that night. He sat on my couch and asked me questions and listened, never telling me what I should and shouldn't do. Even during the whole conversation, when I no longer had anything to hide from him, I was still thinking about when he would leave so I could continue purging all that I had eaten. But he never left, and we both fell asleep on the couch. It grew dark outside, and he rubbed my arm till I opened my eyes slightly. "Babe. It's past midnight. Happy Birthday."

Chapter 28: Rosalina 2.0

Antonio invited me over for a family dinner the following weekend.

"What?" I said.

"Come on, Tony. It's my mom's birthday. It'll be fun! I'm going to cook."

"What did you tell her about me? About us? Hey Mom, this is my friend who I like to roll around with naked ... I'm sure she'd love that."

"Oh God, shut up. I told her that you're my friend, that's it."

"That's it?"

"Please, babe. It means a lot to me," he pleaded, his eyes growing larger.

Antonio insisted that I not bring anything to dinner. Apparently, his mother would be insulted if I showed up with even something as small as cupcakes or fruit. But my mother always said that I couldn't go to someone's house empty handed. I looked outside at the backyard and saw that more roses had bloomed. I grabbed the scissors and walked out the door.

The smell the food wafted into the apartment hallway. My hunger almost outweighed my nerves. Almost.

Antonio opened the door, slipped outside and then shut it. He leaned in and kissed me.

"I just wanted to do that first," he said. He looked down at the roses in my hand. "That's really sweet of you honey. Thank you."

"Tono?" I could hear his mother's voice from behind the door. "Tono? Is he here?" She swung the door open.

"Mommy, this is Tony," Antonio said.

"Hi Tony. Come in." She smiled warmly.

I extended the flowers toward her. "Happy birthday, Ms. Romero."

"Of course. Oh my God, Tony, you're so skinny. Come in and eat!"

"Mommy!" Antonio said, shaking his head.

I returned her smile. "Thank you for having me."

Shit. I still felt validated by comments like hers. *I'm never going to get better.*

The narrow hallway led to a cramped but colourful open living room and kitchen. Pictures of Antonio and Kim were everywhere on the walls and in frames on the side tables. The sun shone through the large window, landing on the varnished parquet floors and numerous glass vases filled with flowers. Antonio's mom put my roses in the middle of the dinner table. "So pretty," she said.

The television—a vintage box-style monitor protruding from the corner of the room—was playing American Idol, or that type of show. In front of the TV were puffy red couches with bright orange crocheted throws.

The apartment was a tidier, more ornate version of Antonio's classroom. A mini kaleidoscope, the brightness even more concentrated here.

We heard the front door open. Kim walked in holding a cake box.

"Are you Tony?" she asked.

"Yes, so nice to meet you."

"I hope you like red velvet." She put the cake into the fridge. "What did you make, Tono?"

"Cornish game hens," he said.

"Cornish game of what? Thrones?" Kim asked.

"It's like chicken, but fancier."

"Wow. We eat'n like white people tonight!" she quipped.

It felt strange saying grace before eating. The last time I'd done that was with my mom.

For several minutes, we ate in silence, broken only by the sound of chewing and of knives scraping the plates.

"This chicken is so good," I said.

"It's Cornish game hen!"

"Sorry."

I turned to Kim. "So, Kim, I hear you'll be applying to universities soon."

"No, colleges."

"What do you want to take?"

"Cosmetology, I think."

"Yeah, but girl, you need to work on those makeup skills, okay?" Antonio said. "You need to finesse that shit up. Less of the makeup, more of the face." He turned to his mother. "We all know she looks like a drag nightmare."

"Shut up!" Kim snapped.

"That's great," I said. "I think George Brown has a good program. Well, at least it did when I was your age, a long time ago, but I don't know now."

"How old *are* you?" Kim asked.

Antonio gasped. "Kim!"

"What?"

"Don't answer that Tony. I'm so sorry," he said.

"It's okay."

Antonio dominated dinner conversation by explaining how he'd prepared the hens. Then he talked about his day in class and how happy he was because one of his students had made a breakthrough by not saying her work was complete shit.

"People need to stop judging the outcomes and just enjoy the process," he said.

As Antonio rambled, I looked over at Kim and their mother. They were hanging on his every word. He could be talking about nothing, and they'd still rise and fall on every sentence, every breath, every inflection. He could splatter paint randomly on any canvas, and they'd think it was a masterpiece. He could lead the most boring class, or put on the worst drag performance, and they'd be amazed. They leaned in, two more sets of pretty hazeley-greyish eyes in front of me; I could recognize Antonio in them, and them in his.

I then remembered that sometimes my mom would look at me with that same attention and what it like was to stare into her eyes and recognize myself in them. It felt like a long time ago.

I looked down at my plate; it was almost clean. The hen was so good I hadn't realized how fast I was inhaling it. I cut another piece and took a bite, and felt a sudden sharp pain on the side of my mouth. I reached up and rubbed my cheek. I could taste blood. I moved my tongue around and felt my tooth wiggle.

"Excuse me," I said as I got up. "Where's your bathroom?"

Antonio looked concerned, whispering, "What are you doing?"

"Nothing."

He looked at me, accusingly.

"I just need to go pee," I mumbled quietly.

In the bathroom, I discovered that one of my bottom right molars had cracked in half. I couldn't see where the fracture was beneath the blood from my gums, but I could feel it with my tongue. The pain was going from throbbing to stinging and back again.

Shit.

After rinsing the blood, I returned to the table and managed to finish the last few pieces of meat, chewing as slowly as I could on the other side of my mouth. I must have looked like a camel. The game hen didn't taste quite the same mixed with blood. But I just kept swallowing the food—and the pain.

His mother looked down at my plate. "Good. Tono, give him more. He's starving," she said.

"No, I'm fine. Really," I said.

"Come on, Tony. You don't need to be shy."

"I should leave room for dessert."

I looked at Antonio for some support. He looked at her. "Rosalinda, don't force him! Jeez!"

"Okay sorry ,Tono."

"Rosalinda?" I asked.

"Yes, when my darling Tono gets mad at me, he calls me by my name," she said.

I chuckled and grinned at Antonio.

After Antonio collected the plates, he leaned down and whispered something in Kim's ear. "We'll be right back," he said, before disappearing with Kim into the hallway. His mom and I were left alone at the table.

"So, Tony. How is your work?" she asked.

"It's okay. I work for a marketing and consulting firm."

"I know."

"You do?"

"Yeah. Tono told me. He told me everything about you."

"Everything?"

"Yeah."

"Oh." I felt like sinking into my chair.

She looked over at the roses.

"The roses are beautiful. I'm so glad you didn't kill that garden completely," she said.

I felt the room get warmer and sank lower in my chair. I wanted to shrink now more than ever. "Um ... Antonio's an amazing gardener—I can't believe he was able to save it. Did he get that from—"

She interrupted me. "He's been so happy since he met you, you know? Thank you."

I didn't know what to say. "Same with me, he's a great guy," was the best I could come up with. Sweat dripped down my armpits.

Antonio and Kim came back from the hallway carrying a large canvas with a red bow on top, hiding the front side from us. "You ready?"

"Oh Dios mio, Tono, what is that?" his mother asked.

Antonio flipped it around. It was the portrait of her from the classroom. "Do you like it?"

Her eyes widened, and then began to well. "Thank you, hijo. I love it. It's beautiful ..." She tilted her face upward and brought a hand to her cheek. "Oh my, I'm beautiful."

Kim rolled her eyes. "And here we go."

"Maybe we should hang it at the front entrance ..." his mother said.

"See, what did I tell you, Tony?" Antonio fell into hysterical laughter.

His mother got up and walked back toward the kitchen. "Celos! You're just jealous, Tono."

After two slices of the red velvet cake (the sugar in the icing was the only thing stronger than the taste of my bloody cracked tooth), Antonio brought me to his room. I sat on his tiny bed—it was a single. "How do you fit on this?" I chuckled.

"I don't," he replied. "I've had this bed since I was a kid. My feet now hang over the edge."

He walked over to his closet and pulled out a beaded, sequined red gown. "I think I'm gonna wear this for the big pageant."

"Pageant?" I asked.

"The Miss Magic Mirror pageant. At the Flamingo. I told you about this last week."

"You did?"

"Yeah! It's on August eighth—two weeks from now."

"I'm sorry, I don't remember."

Antonio shook his head. "Anyway, it's only like the biggest drag competition in the city. It's my big shot. No more substitute hosting—that show will be all mine every night. Plus the cash prize. I'll be able to buy more supplies for the class, maybe get some proper brushes and easels that don't tip over. If I can't get into the arts school in Montreal, at least I'll have this. Get me some proper makeup for my drag. This shit from the dollar store's giving me more itch than a yeast infection."

We laughed. He sat beside me on the bed and ran his hand over my shoulder and down my back. "I'm glad you're here."

"Me too," I said. "I didn't know your family called you Tono."

"Yeah, makes me feel like a kid again."

He leaned in and kissed me. I kept my mouth closed so he wouldn't taste the blood.

"Wait," I said. "What *did* you tell your mom about us?"

His face melted into a big, dimpled smile. "I told her everything. Everything about us." He looked like he might burst into tears of joy.

"Everything?"

"Yeah."

"That's amazing. Oh my God." I kissed him.

"I even told her about my drag."

"How'd she feel about that?"

"Well, my drag name is her name. She loves herself, so she loves Rosalinda." He laughed.

"She loves you more though."

"I know." He got up and put the dress back in the closet. "We should get back downstairs. They'll probably think we're doing it in here."

Before I left, Antonio's mother handed me a plastic bag. "Here, take some of the chicken."

"It's a Cornish game hen!" Antonio yelled. "Oh Dios mio,

Rosalinda!"

She ignored him. "And some more cake. Please."

"Thank you, Ms. Romero."

"You can call me Tita."

"Okay, Tita."

I smiled as I waited for the elevator. Tita means the same in Spanish as it does in Tagalog: "Auntie."

I got home and despite the pain in my mouth and having gulped down my own blood for the last few hours, I still wanted to eat. Meeting Antonio's family was a big deal. But I'd made it through.

I devoured the food his mother had packed for me, chewing on the good side of my mouth. I grew impatient and started swallowing faster, chewing less. When I got to the cake, I just swirled it around my tongue and forced it down my throat. The gum beneath my cracked tooth must have begun to clot since I wasn't tasting the blood as much anymore.

Then of course, I needed to get rid of it. I needed to erase what I had just done. Press the restart button. I went to the bathroom and threw up as much as I could. The vomit—including three slices of red velvet cake—mixed with the blood from my tooth made my toilet bowl look like a murder scene.

Yet again, I had killed the very little progress I had made. But with each flush the evidence vanished, just as I had flushed the food from my system.

I went downstairs to grab my phone from my jacket pocket. Five missed calls, all of them from Antonio.

Shit.

I cleared my throat and dialed his number.

He picked up. "Hey."

"Hi. Sorry I missed your calls."

"I wanted to make sure you got home okay."

"Thanks, I did. That was a great night. Your mom and sister are so sweet."

"They really liked you."

"I liked them too."

Silence.

"Tony?" he said.

"Yeah?"

"Were you in the bathroom when I was calling?"

"No. No, of course not. I just forgot my phone was in my jacket."

Silence.

"Yeah, you were. I know what you were doing," he said.

I couldn't lie again.

"Tony?"

"Yeah."

"I made that food for you."

"I'm sorry. I told you this is tough for me."

"I gotta go," he said.

Call ended, my phone read.

I sent an "I'm so sorry" text and then took my medication. He didn't reply.

I'd have to book a dentist appointment as soon as I could. But then I remembered my benefits only covered eighty percent of all procedures, and I would have to go back into overdraft if I had to cover the rest.

Chapter 29: Blank Canvas

The next day, I sent a few text messages to Antonio:

> *I'm sorry Antonio. I didn't mean to upset you.*

No response.

Another try:

> *It's me again. Can you just let me know that you get this?*

His reply:

Got it.

> *How are you? Are you still upset with me?*

I'm about to watch Ru-Paul's Drag Race. I'll be in a better mood in an hour.

I smiled. At least I knew he could still joke with me. I texted him the lines from the Anne Sexton poem:

> *you powdered your sorrow, you gave it a back rub*
>
> *and then you covered it with a blanket*
>
> *and after it had slept a while it woke*
>
> *to the wings of the roses and was transformed*

He wrote back:

I'm sorry too. Let's talk after class tomorrow.

After my class the next day, I went to Antonio's classroom. He stood at the front with his back toward me, painting what looked like a wolf, over top of a painting of another animal.

"Hi," I said softly.

He turned around. He smiled shyly, and then turned back to his painting. "Hi."

"You're painting over another painting?"

"Yeah. I can't get it right. It was supposed to be a wolf, but ended up looking like a bitch. So I decided just to paint over it."

"You can do that?"

"What?"

"Paint over another painting?"

"Yeah why not. It's easier to improve something that already exists. Same thing in writing, right?"

"What do you mean?"

"Isn't writing also rewriting, in addition to writing from scratch?"

"You're right."

"Plus, blank canvases scare me," he said. "It's like the potential to screw up the perfect vision I have in my head is staring me in the face."

I nodded.

He continued. "The only thing with repaints is that when you get close to it, you can see all the bumps and cracks underneath."

"Maybe it gives it character?"

"Maybe."

Silence.

"I'm sorry, Antonio."

He put the brush down. "I'm sorry too. I just got so upset."

"No, I understand that."

"I just want you to get better. That's all. It's just hard to watch and feel like you can't help."

"I know. It's a process." I wanted to say, "it's a process you shouldn't have to watch me go through," but I didn't.

"Are you heading out soon?"

"Why?"

"I want to take you somewhere."

"You gonna blindfold me again?"

"Ha. No."

"So where?"

"Well, I got to meet your mom, right?"

The cemetery was about twenty minutes from my house. Even though my mother was a devout Catholic, I'd decided on a cemetery for all different faiths. By the time she died, I had become more of an atheist, so it didn't really matter.

"Her headstone is beautiful," Antonio said.

I went with a light pink stone, with a floral pattern on the top and down the sides. Below her name was a small portrait stuck onto stone—the image was from a family wedding she and I had attended in the Philippines back when I was fourteen. She looked so happy and healthy, nothing like when she was sick. For months—no, years—after she died, I couldn't see her as her healthy self when I thought of her. The sick version of her—the eighty pounds of her, the bald head, the pale skin, the sunken, jaundiced eyes, the hollow cheeks, the protruding collar bones and spine, the ribs on top of the concave stomach, the constantly shivering hands, and so on and so on—had cemented itself in my memory. It was a while before I noticed that I was envisioning what she looked like when she *wasn't* sick whenever I thought of her.

Antonio looked at the neighbouring spaces. "Oh look, your mom is beside a little Chinese lady. So sweet. I bet they get lots of manicures together. And on the other side ... oh ... a man. He's Spanish!" He looked closer at the photo. "Handsome. At least momma's got some eye candy."

He bent to get closer to the ground. "Let's get cozy," he said.

He plopped down on the ground and lay on his back, his head close to the headstone.

"What are you doing?" I asked. "You're lying on top of her."

"No, honey. She's in a fancy box lined with silk. She's good." He looked up at the light blue sky. The sun was blinding.

"You'll hurt your eyes looking into the sun like that. Don't you have sunglasses?" I asked.

"Nah. I don't want a barrier."

"You look like a crazy person right now."

"Thanks. You gonna join me?"

"Why?"

"We can watch the clouds roll by together."

I looked around to see if there was anyone else nearby.

"Come on, Tony. Lie with me."

"Fine. But I feel stupid." I lay down beside him. "So we're just going to lie here?"

"That's right."

I took a deep breath, inhaling the quiet.

"It's relaxing, isn't it?"

"Yeah."

A cloud sailed over to right and covered up the sun. I opened my eyes fully.

"Sometimes it's good to just look up at the sky," Antonio said. "You know, remind yourself of how small you are. We're just little nothings ... specks of dust. And the sky can just swallow us up at any second."

The cloud moved on. I closed my eyes, feeling the sun on my eyelids. And then something grabbed my hand.

It was Antonio's hand.

I peeked over at him. He had his eyes closed too. He was biting his lower lip.

He opened his eyes, raised his eyebrows and smiled back at me. "You know when a moment feels so good, you gotta bite something?"

"Sure."

But suddenly the moment didn't feel so good for me.

How can someone love another person, and at the same time, possibly ruin that person's life with their own problems? How could I be with Antonio, without being a burden on him? How could anyone with illness *not* be a burden, despite how much love there is? I loved my mother, but I felt angry too, as if she was one.

How could I even think that?

"I hope you have a lot of those good moments in your life," I said to Antonio. But I wasn't sure if he'd have them if I was around, clouding his vast, sunny—and seemingly limitless—sky.

Chapter 30: Clouds Descend

I don't deserve Antonio.

Grindr. 6:38 p.m.

What u into?
Whatever.
Really?
Yeah.
...
What are you into?
everything. Oral. Anal. U a bottom?
Yeah.
Makes sense.
Why do you say that?
Not so much yellow tops out there
I mean not so much Asian tops out there

6:47 p.m.

Chapter 30: Clouds Descend

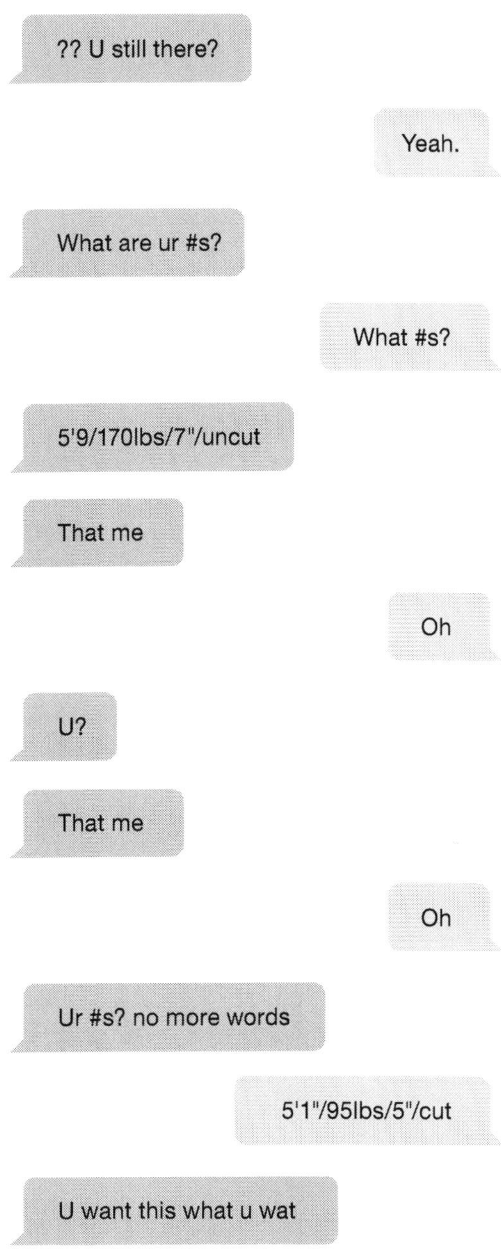

<He sent a picture of his genitals.>

Thx.

Is that a yes??

Yes.

U sure u can take this?

Yes.

Call me sir.

Yes sir.

Good boy.

U have pics?

Yes.

Send

<He sent a picture of his genitals.>

You send me one of your face first.

No more words, send pics

I wanna see you ass now

Nvm. Gotta go.

Hold on. here.

<He sent a picture of a man with a beard.>

Now send me pic

Of my face?

No. don't care abt face. Send me ur ass

<I sent a picture of my butt.>

Nice.

U open minded boy?

Yes.

U sure u open minded?

Yes.

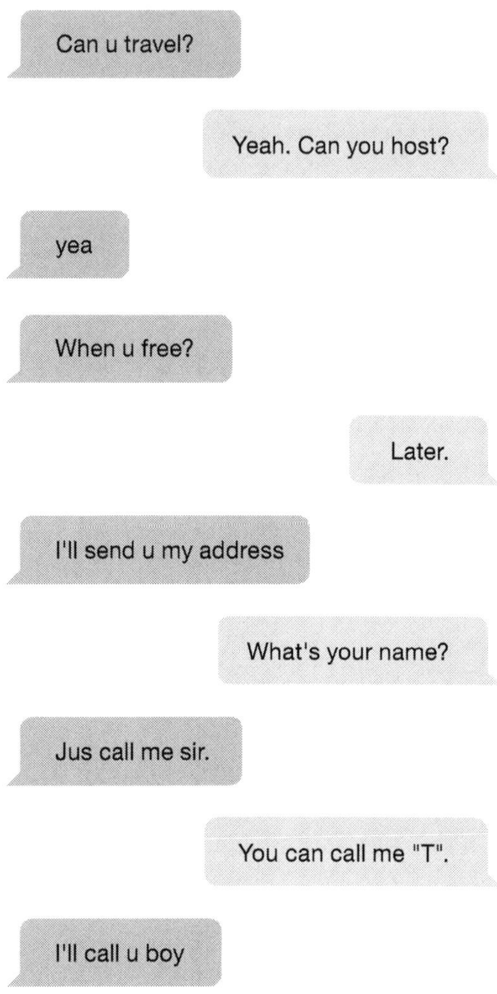

Sir lived uptown in the Annex, in one of the newer buildings. I parked a couple of blocks away so he wouldn't see my car.

12:42am

"What suite you going to?" the security guard asked.

"1005."

The guard made a quick call and then buzzed me in.

I looked in the elevator mirror. My eyes and cheeks looked more sunken in. I always thought top lighting made me look my best.

I got off the elevator and walked to door 1005. I stood there for a few seconds.

Wait.

What am I doing?

Just as I was about to turn back, the door opened. "Come in, boy."

I walked in. Even through the dim lights, it was apparent that Sir was wealthy. The floors were marble, and the hallway console table looked like it was from one of those pricey furniture stores on King Street.

I looked up to see his face, but he immediately grabbed my head and turned it away. "Don't look at my face boy."

"What?"

"You said you were open minded, right?"

"Yeah."

"So then you'll do what I say."

"Okay."

"Okay what? What did I tell you to call me?"

"Okay Sir."

"Good. Now follow me."

He put his hand on the back of my neck and led me to the bathroom. He had a few candles burning. The lights were off.

"Look down," he said.

I looked down. He walked in circles around me a couple of times.

"You're dirty," he said. "Take your clothes off."

"You don't want to talk first, maybe?"

"Talk? Why?"

He walked away and turned the shower on. I could see he was wearing a bathrobe. He took it off and stood in front of me. I was too scared to look at his face, so I kept my head down, managing a couple of peeks at his body. White hairs were scattered among the dark ones on his chest.

This man was older. Much older than Antonio, probably me too. Old enough that his life couldn't be ruined by me, by anything anymore.

"I told you to take your clothes off. Never mind, I'll do it."

He turned me around and undressed me, then led me into the steaming shower.

"Turn around and get on your knees."

I stood like a frightened child.

"Fuck, just do it."

I knelt, and the hot water ran down my head and my back. "So dirty," he said again. I felt shampoo drip onto my head, followed by his hands in my hair. He washed my head for what felt like fifteen minutes.

"Can I get up now?" I asked

"No. You're going to stay right there."

He finished rinsing off my head. He pressed his hand against the back of my neck, pushing me down. "Lower boy," he said.

My face was near my knees now. The glass doors of the shower were completely fogged. I saw the tops of his feet behind me. I felt the water on my back ... then I saw the stream leading to the drain turn yellow. I shut my eyes, so the urine wouldn't get in them, and waited till it was over.

"You're so dirty, boy," he said. He shampooed my hair again.

"You want to fuck me boy?" he asked.

"Sorry, but no, Sir."

"What?"

What am I doing? "You know what? I gotta go. I'm can't do this. I'm sorry." I ran out of the shower and frantically pulled on my clothes. I could feel his stare singe my back. "Thank you," I said, running out the door.

The water, soaked through my clothes and dripping, left a trail from the elevator to the front door. I pretended not to hear the security guard saying goodnight.

I don't remember much else from that night, which is a good thing.

On the drive home, I thought about how nice it would be to be a robot. To not feel pain or sadness. To feel nothing. To not think. To quantify, and cut. To not bleed. To not be able to remember.

I don't deserve Antonio anyway.

I'd like to be a robot. Mostly because I'd like to have an off button.

Chapter 31: Miss Magic Mirror

Antonio was always a confident person, but the night of the Miss Magic Mirror pageant brought out an unhinged and jittery child. At one point he even said he felt like throwing up. Then, "Oh, sorry, Tony. You know I didn't mean anything by that."

"Maybe you should throw up. Maybe your dress will fit better," I said.

"How can you say something like that?" he said, appalled.

"Come on, at least let me make fun of it."

"That's messed up."

We stood in the backstage dressing room of the White Flamingo, crammed with five other drag queens, feverishly applying makeup with fifteen minutes to go before show time. Each drag queen's mirror and desk was a pile of makeup, glitter and other random items: panty hose, eyelash glue, sparkle nail polish, duct tape.

"Hand me my lipstick," Antonio said.

"Which one? You have a ton of them in this bag," I said, shuffling through the tubes.

"The sienna sunset."

"By sienna sunset, I assume you mean red?"

I handed him one of the tubes. He pulled off the top. "No, find the one that looks like the sunset—like a bit brighter ... never mind."

"Aren't all the lipsticks the same?" I asked.

Three of the drag queens turned around and looked at me with disgust. "Excuuuse me? Did you just say all the lipsticks are the same?" one queen named Mother Trinidad asked in outrage.

"Oh, no she didn't!" Another queen—Chichi—snapped.

"Sorry, ladies," I said.

"All you boyz sayin' you sorry but we all know dat shii just comes out yo mouth like fuckin bubbles," Mother Trinidad said.

"Pop!" Chichi said.

Mother Trinidad was a veteran drag queen. She was over six feet tall, with legs for days. She had started doing drag as soon as she left Trinidad and Tobago as a teenager over ten years ago, and she called her performances a tribute to her home country. She wore a disco-inspired strapless fuchsia dress, matched by fuchsia earrings, fuchsia eyeshadow and eight-inch fuchsia heels. Her huge fluffy hair got caught in one of the dim light bulbs overhead. "Oh, child, my head's gon catch fire. There must be a priest in da house!" she yelled, and everyone cackled with laughter.

The favourite to win the crown was Chichi, a Filipino queen who, like Antonio, had hosted a few events at the Flamingo to rave reviews. She also was a regular performer at a couple of smaller gay bars in the village and on Queen West. She was a self-proclaimed "no nonsense bitch that likes to make money ... I like to make men run for their money and I don't feel bad because I am tired of being run by men." She said that line at an event the previous month, and the crowd had cheered in a frenzy.

Chichi walked over to Antonio as he applied his lipstick. Twirling with her blonde braids, which were woven with pink and black ribbon, between her long pink acrylic nails, she leaned into the mirror and put her face close to Antonio's: "Girl, your hair is whack. You got a rat's nest on your head. Let me fix it now!"

"Thanks, Chichi," Antonio said, handing her a brush.

Another queen—called Keri Hussle, dressed in a retro waitress uniform—went to Mother Trinidad and Chichi in a panic: "Girls, could you lend me some blush? I'm out."

"Hell no Miss Thang!" Mother Trinidad yelled. "This is a competition! You should have brought your own!"

Keri gasped and put her hand to her mouth in disbelief.

"Oh please, Queen, don't play dramatic Miss Innocent with me," Mother Trinidad scolded.

"Here. Help yourself," Chichi said, throwing a makeup bag at her.

"Thank you, Chichi! You're a life saver!" Keri said.

"You know, Chichi, dis ain't the Miss Congeniality convention. Dis here is a beauty pageant. All bitches for demselves!" Mother Trinidad said.

"Oh shut your hole, the flies are getting in," Chichi snapped.

"Ladies, your fighting is hurting my chakra!" Antonio said.

"Your what? Are you talking about your coochie, baby girl?" Chichi asked, giggling. "Look now, Rosalinda, your hair is perfect." She turned Antonio back to the mirror.

"That looks amazing, thank you!"

"Honey, you're lucky I'm not charging," Chichi said, walking away, "I'd charge you for something else though."

The show was starting in five minutes. "I should get to my seat babe," I said. "Your mom and your sister should be here by now. Good luck, beautiful!" All the drag queens looked over at us.

"All of you are beautiful," I said.

"Mmhmm," Mother Trinidad snarled. I turned around and left the dressing room.

Antonio's mother and sister were sitting in second row, all the way to the side.

"Tony, so nice to see you again," his mother said. "We have to have you at the house again soon."

"Of course, Ms. Romero." I said.

"It's Tita."

"Right! Tita." I smiled.

Kim sat beside her, texting on her phone. She looked up, hugged me and whispered, "sorry that I said you were old at dinner." I giggled. She sat back down and went right back to her phone.

I took a seat beside his mother. I felt a tap on my shoulder. I turned to see Nick, Lisa, Ben and Kevin sitting behind me.

"Gettin cozy with the in-laws, I see," Nick whispered, laughing under his breath.

Soon the bar was packed.

The contest had two rounds—a lip-sync performance and an interview question. The winner would get the regular gig of hosting all the White Flamingo's events for a year starting in the fall—such as the weekly Best Ass contest, the Twink Tuesdays dance party, and Leather-Bound Sundays—plus the opportunity to host events for a charity of their choice. On top of all this, there was a cash prize of a thousand dollars, and a year's supply of Magic Mirror makeup.

To the left of the stage were the judges—the bar's owner, some Magic Mirror executive and another drag queen who had won the contest a few years before.

The reigning Miss Magic Mirror White Flamingo was Dairy Kween, who had grown up in Nappanee raising cows—hence her name. She had been praised in the last year for bringing her self-proclaimed hill-billy, white-trash sense of humour. She had worked across Toronto lending her talents to the Safeway House, a charity supporting homeless youth.

The lights dimmed—the competition was beginning. After telling a few jokes, thanking the sponsors and introducing the judges, Dairy Kween called out the first performer for the lip-sync round.

Mother Trinidad performed to the gay anthem "I Will Survive" by Gloria Gaynor, delighting the older folks in the crowd. Antonio said the key to a successful drag performance was to have a certain moment during the song, something unique the audience would remember after the performance. You could call it a schtick, a gimmick ... whatever. Mother Trinidad's moment was when her many beaded necklaces exploded at the song's crescendo. The beads—silver, pink, blue, red—flew from her neck, bouncing and rolling off the stage.

Chichi came out in a frayed denim vest with silver buttons and a tight jean skirt cut off at the waistband. Her provocative grinding to Khia's explicit "My Neck, My Back"—along with her skirt riding up her butt to show her hot pink thong—stunned the audience into silence; she was phenomenal. But just as she looked ready to run away with the competition based on this performance alone, she stumbled on a few silver beads from Mother Trinidad's necklace. Her feet flew out from under her, and in an almost acrobatic move, she flew across the stage and fell onto her face. The crowd cheered when she got up and continued to perform despite a bloody knee.

"Oh Dios mio," Ms. Romero said. "These guys are amazing. Did Tono practice enough?"

"I'm sure he did," I said. I started to panic too. I hadn't seen Antonio practice at all.

Dairy Kween then announced the next contestant: "Everybody, welcome our little spicy taco ... Rosalinda!" We all cheered.

Rosalinda strutted out in her red beaded dress. Rhianna's "We Found Love" blasted, his gyrating hips moving in perfect unison with the beats, exciting the crowd. He did this move where he appeared to walk and dance under an invisible limbo stick, lower and lower, to the point where I feared his seven-inch stilettos would cave under him. But they never did. He ended the performance jumping and landing in perfect splits. He had nailed it. His mother and Kim clapped in relief and pride.

Chichi's fall and bloody knee landed her in the lead after the lip-sync round. Rosalinda was second, and Mother Trinidad was third.

As with all pageants, the question round—which only the top three after the lip-synch would move on to—was notorious for stumping even the wittiest of queens. Previous questions had been philosophical, political or even esoteric:

"Are drag queens born or raised?"

"What's the biggest socio-political crisis of the drag community right now?"

"What is your essence?"

Antonio said the key to a successful pageant interview was to say something meaningful, funny or crass, and memorable. And the delivery was just as important. Confident but not arrogant. Sassy but not obnoxious. The year before, Dairy Kween had won by saying her "essence" was that of the cows she raised on the farm: "I live life like a cow grazes … slowly and surely, to have a taste of everything. Plus, I like being milked."

In random order, Mother Trinidad was up first, while Chichi and Antonio and were brought offstage to avoid hearing the question.

As the lights lowered and the dramatic thumping music played like on Miss Universe—Dairy Kween read the final question off her cue card: "What is the most important quality that Miss Magic Mirror should have?"

The question seemed less frightening than in previous years. Regardless, Ms. Romero leaned over and whispered in my ear, "Oh shit."

Mother Trinidad immediately responded. "Self-confidence." A few whistles and "Yes Queen!"s were heard from the audience. She then grabbed the microphone and turned it into a TED Talk: "Y'alls gots to have some self-confidence and show 'em who's boss. Cuz if you don't, people will walk all over you! Miss Magic Mirror must be strong, and bold and fabulous, and … well, y'all know I am ready to slay all that." The crowd cheered and clapped.

Chichi limped up to the stage, blood soaking through her

bandaged knee. As soon as the question music started to play, she leaned into the microphone and said, "Dairy Kween, now don't be asking me some philosophical shit, like what colour is my aura, okay?" The crowed howled.

"I'll tell you what, Chichi, you can show me the colour of your aura backstage after the show, okay, honey?" Dairy Kween quipped.

"Thank you."

"Okay, now for the question. What is the most important quality that Miss Magic Mirror should have?"

Chichi took the microphone and looked out into audience.

"A quality? Miss Magic Mirror should be smart enough know where the money at."

The crowd reacted with mostly cheers and laughter, but also a couple of boos.

"What?" she continued. "It's just the truth. Chichi always said, if it ain't tight, it ain't right!" The audience laughed and then hollered.

Ms. Romero and Kim looked at each other, worried. Both Mother Trinidad and Chichi had more than confidently nailed the confidence bit.

I tried to ease their worries: "That all sounded good, but really it was all catch phrases and clichés. Meant nothing."

They didn't look convinced. I wasn't good at convincing myself either, even though I thought both answers sounded like sassy Hallmark-card memes. But would the judges fall for it?

"All right ladies and ladies," Dairy Kween huffed. "I'm tired and ready to take the girls out, you know what I'm saying? Bring out that bitch for our final question—Rosalinda."

I could feel my heart beating slower with each step Antonio took toward centre stage.

"Okay, Rosalinda. The final question is—"

Suddenly I could taste blood in my mouth. *Fuck, this stupid cracked tooth.* I still hadn't gone to the dentist.

"What is the most important quality that Miss Magic Mirror should have?"

Oddly, the taste of blood woke up my taste buds. I was starving; the blood's rustiness was the first thing I had tasted in almost ten hours.

Antonio paused and looked around. I wasn't sure if he had drawn a blank and was looking to stall, or if he hadn't heard the question. His eyes continued to scan the room, stopping on Ms. Romero and me.

I heard a whisper. "Give me your hand." It was Ms. Romero's voice. I felt her fingers clutch my palm, and then squeeze harder.

Antonio leaned into the microphone. "Empathy."

"Empathy?" Dairy Kween asked.

"Yes. I think Miss Magic Mirror should be able to walk in someone else's shoes—and not just heels, of course. Everybody approaches life from their own narrow point of view. But to live what other people go through and feel their joy and pain and to share in it ... it may not solve the problem, but it makes people feel less lonely. And I think that is magical."

The crowd was quiet. The judges stared at each other.

Five minutes later, Ms. Romero was sobbing in my arms as Antonio walked to the corners of the stage with the crown on his head.

The bar had almost cleared out. Most of the drag queens had left except for Mother Trinidad, who was now completely drunk and cursing loudly: "That Salty Taco, Rosa-fuck'n-Linda—she only won cuz they ain't had a Latino win in like ten years. Fuck affirmative action!"

Chichi rolled her eyes. "We're all minorities, you stupid bitch!"

I went into the dressing room. For days, I had been gathering the courage to say what I needed to. I wasn't sure if it would ever come.

Had I lost courage—along with everything else—with all the food I had purged over the years?

Antonio had read my mind with his answer. Empathy. If I were in his shoes with a bright future, I wouldn't want anything holding me back.

Quantify, Cut. Just be a robot, Tony. Just feel nothing.

"Oh my God! Tony! I can't believe it!" Antonio screamed, running into my arms. "I could not have done this without you."

"This was all you. You deserve this."

He leapt up into my arms.

"I need to tell you something," I said, not making eye contact.

He interrupted. "I love you, Tony."

"What?"

"I said I love you."

I forced a smile, speechless. I couldn't say this to him now. I couldn't tell him and spoil his night.

"I gotta go. You go enjoy this win. Everyone is waiting for you at the bar," I said before I kissed him.

"Wait, where you going?" he asked as I turned and walked away. Chichi ran into the dressing room, grabbed him and spun him around: "Condragulations honey!"

I walked faster as he kept calling for me, trying to shut the sound of his voice out of my ears.

Chapter 32: Black Canvas

Your voice still rings in my ears, but this time I'm wide awake.

That night, I found myself standing in my backyard with a shovel, an axe and a bottle of bleach. It was one in the morning. I couldn't sleep.

"Don't kill my roses."

Why? Do I have to take care of them because you once did? To not waste all your long and hard hours of work? To not let something die just because it's beautiful? Why do I owe this to you? I don't owe you anything. It was not my choice to inherit this. You didn't even ask me. You just came, dug holes in the ground, planted your flowers and then left. Why do I have to care for this because you can't?

The first swing with the axe made a loud snapping sound followed by the leaves shaking. A bunch of red petals flew in the air.

"Don't kill my roses."

I know what the roses represent. A life you have created for me ... a promise that I will grow and bloom? You made me promise to do this. But you're not here—you didn't keep your promise.

Three, four, five more swings and I was almost done the first flower bed. My axe was too dull. I went back into the house to get the big shears. The screeching of the blades like music to my ears.

Sweat dripped from my head and neck and down my back as I dug up the ground, axed and snipped off the thick vines, finishing it off by pouring the bleach in the holes. Each ripped-out root filled the holes in me with satisfaction. Each drop of bleach melting into the earth soothed my anxiety.

An hour later, I was happy with my progress. The flowers now looked like dead bodies, floating, with their heads cut off.

Quantify, cut, kill.

There is no chance for the roses to die anymore.

When it was done, I threw the tools and the bottle aside, and, just as Antonio and I had done at Mom's grave, lay on the ground and looked up into the dark sky. If only I too could sink into the dirt, or have the sky swallow me up.

My heartbeat slowed, and my vision got lost in the black canvas above me. A few stars were sailing slowly to the right, signalling that the sky was moving and at some point the sun would reappear for another day.

Should reappear.

"Don't kill my roses."

There was no point in keeping them alive. One day those flowers would have died; this garden, this grass … I … will all die. You already did.

So don't be upset with me for delaying the inevitable. Maybe now I'll stop hearing your voice.

Chapter 33: Memory, Please Fail Me

I heard the whispering of familiar voices. I opened my eyes and saw Lisa and Nick standing at the sides of my bed. But it wasn't my bed. The sheets didn't feel so soft. I wasn't wearing my clothes. The gown I was wearing was paper thin. This wasn't home.

Nick and Lisa noticed my eyes were open and stopped whispering to each other.

"Tony, buddy. How are you feeling?" Nick asked.

I moved to get myself upright, and the bed beneath me shook. Or it felt like it. My head fell back, hitting the pillow, my vision whirling in circles as if I was on a carousel. I reached down the side of bed to ground myself when I felt a stinging pain in my forearm. I realized I was attached to an IV. I automatically tugged at the clear tape on the needle and tube; Nick grabbed my hand to stop me.

"No, Tony. Don't do that or else it'll come out."

I couldn't talk but rather grunted at Nick to leave me alone. Lisa looked on, worried. A nurse walked into the room.

"What's happening?" she asked.

"He's trying to pull his IV out," Lisa said.

"Tony, calm down," the nurse said, as she forced my hand away from my arm. "Calm down." She was surprisingly strong for a small Asian woman. A doctor came in as I thrashed around in the bed and restrained me, while telling Nick to back away.

"Can we get him an Ativan?" the doctor said.

"Right away."

Suddenly my arms and eyelids felt heavy and I couldn't fight them anymore.

"Good job … just relax, boss," his warm voice soothed.

And then the black canvas slowly took over my sight.

I opened my eyes and saw Nick and Lisa standing at the sides of my bed. This wasn't my bed, or sheets, or clothes. *Déjà vu.*

Fuck, I really am here.

Nick and Lisa stood by and watched as the doctor filled me in on the details of how I'd arrived at the emergency room: that Antonio had found me in my backyard after I hadn't been responding to his texts, that my iron and potassium levels were deathly low, that I was severely dehydrated, that the blood in my mouth was from a bottom molar was severely cracked, and other things I couldn't take in at the moment.

"Tony, after you stabilize, I want you to think about what you're going to do after we release you," the doctor said. "Dr. Tee faxed over your referral forms for St. Paul's. Do you remember him telling you about that place?"

I nodded. The place where you have to eat.

"You really to need consider that. But nobody can force you to go. You have to decide for yourself."

Nick and Lisa stayed in the room with me for another hour. Lisa got on the bed beside me and placed my head on her shoulder. Nick sat on a chair, holding my hand. We didn't talk. But with each rub on my shoulder and stroke on my arm I was reminded of what I had been forgetting: they were my family. They loved me.

I was an asshole. How could I forget what I should be grateful for?

They left and assured me that they'd be back tomorrow. I wanted to ask them to promise, but didn't. I had put them through so much already.

I spent the next couple of hours falling in and out of sleep. Then, when the cloudiness in my head subsided, I read the pamphlets about St. Paul's that the doctor had left on my side table.

The nurse told me there was a visitor. Antonio cautiously walked in, his eyes wide open. He was holding red tulips.

"Hi. I thought these might remind you of that tulips poem by Sylvia Plath you like so much."

"Thanks. That poem is about her being in the hospital resenting the vibrant red tulips because they remind her of what it felt to be alive ... but she just wants to die."

"Oh. Shit, sorry."

I smiled. "Interpretations are subjective. The tulips are beautiful. Thank you."

He placed them on the table and sat on the chair beside my bed, his face filled with concern, and anger. "What were you thinking?"

"I'm sorry. I didn't mean to kill your roses."

"I don't care about the roses."

"Why aren't you wearing your crown?" I asked, trying to lighten the mood.

"This isn't time for jokes."

"Sorry."

"Don't apologize to me. Apologize to yourself. Look what you're doing to yourself."

I looked away.

"Sorry," he said. "I didn't mean to come here to upset you."

"It's okay. You're right."

"You never told me what you were going to say that night."

"What?"

"After the pageant. You said you wanted to tell me something."

Then I remembered.

I didn't need to feel courageous this time to tell him what I wanted to say. It was too hard and exhausting to feel courageous. I was already at the bottom to fall any further. I had nothing to lose. I felt relief.

"Remember when I said that the secret to happiness was to lower your standards?" I asked.

"Yeah."

"Forget that. Don't lower them."

"Okay ..."

"I was wrong. Don't settle for just whatever. You have so much going for you, Antonio. You can have whatever you want because you have talent and you're a good person. You have your whole life ahead of you. Just like you said, right? Find hope for something in the future, and then work toward it."

"Well, thank you. But where's this coming from?"

"I've just been thinking about things. About us."

"Okay. What are you telling me?"

Just feel nothing. Be a robot.

"I can't spoil things for you anymore. You need to move on. I need to move on."

"No."

I shook my head.

"What do you want me to do?" he asked.

"Just go. Move on. You have so many big things waiting for you."

"What about you?"

I took a breath. "I'm going to check into this program at St. Paul's. Maybe I can get better. I don't know if that will happen, but I have to at least try."

"How long is the program?"

"Three months."

"I'll wait for you, Tony. Then we can start over. I'll wait for you."

"Don't. Promise me you won't do that."

"I meant what I said at the bar that night."

I love you. He said "I love you" that night.

"I know you did. I love you too. That's why you can't wait for me."

He stared at me for what felt like hours, to which I couldn't keep eye contact and looked away. He kissed me, reminding me of that trace of that birthday cake scent which he left lingering. As he walked out of the hospital room, I wanted to memorize how handsome he was, how even brighter his hazeley-greyish eyes were as he looked at me longingly that one last time. How his wavy hair framed his big shiny smile and how a few of his curls bounced when he walked. I wanted to memorize how beautiful he'd looked the night before with his red dress and crown on his head. But then I realized how these memories might follow and haunt me later—forcing me to think of fonder times and *long* for them, just like all the other ones did, and so I shut my eyes and tried to rid my head of the images with a long exhale.

Memory, please fail me.

Part Three

Chapter 34: Welcome to St. Paul's

"Here's the nurses' station, which overlooks the main lobby," Gladys, the nurse on duty, said to Lisa and me during my welcome tour. There was a group of patients gathered around the front desk, mumbling to each other.

"Don't mind them," Gladys said. "All the patients like to see the new residents coming in. Or the guests visiting them. They'll take any chance to get a glimpse outside the facility." Some of the patients looked like skeletons, sitting in wheelchairs as nurses glided them from one area to the next.

The seventh floor walls of St. Paul's were bare and grey, stripped of any pictures, posters or signs, each corner holding a dispenser of hand sanitizer. As Lisa and I walked behind Gladys, I began losing track of where we were and what we had already seen; it was a maze of identically sterile squares.

The nurses physically mirrored the place, dressed in grey scrubs, blending into the walls. They floated around the floor like sharks, some smiling and some not, quietly, until they presented small paper cups of pills and water for the patients to swallow as they observed. Some nurses asked the patients to open their mouths afterward, to make sure the pills were gone.

Lisa sensed that I was getting overwhelmed. She grabbed my

hand. "It's okay. You'll be fine."

"This hall leads to the cafeteria, where we eat three times a day. You get snacks throughout and you can take those back to your room if you want," Gladys said. We walked further down the hallway, the clicking of Lisa's heels echoing. "And around the corners are the bathrooms."

The bathrooms. The elusive hidden spaces that were locked for two hours after every meal and 30 minutes after snack time.

We ended the tour in my room. Gladys turned to me, looking earnest. "So, you'll have to get used to this, but you always have to keep your door open."

"Okay," I nodded.

"I let you get settled in," Gladys said, leaving Lisa and me alone in my room.

Lisa walked over to the window. "You have a nice view of the ... parking lot."

"Thanks," I said, looking around the room. "Oh God, this place is hideous. Lisa, what did I do?"

"You'll be fine, it'll just take some time to get used to. You've already done the hardest part by coming here," she said, trying to sound reassuring.

"Right."

"If I don't make it back later today, I'll be here tomorrow for sure, okay?"

"It's okay."

"I brought you some pillow-y slippers ... it might make you feel more at home." She left a plastic Wal-Mart bag on top of my bag.

I spent a half-hour after she left staring out the window. The parking lot was for visitors. I watched a couple of people park and then sit in their cars for a minute or two before getting out. Then I saw people walk to their cars after their visit, and similarly sit for some time in the driver's seat before pulling out of the lot and driving back to their real lives. One man held his face in his hands and cried for a full minute before wiping it with tissue and starting the engine.

253

"Tony, lunch will be served in fifteen minutes," Gladys said.

I always heard that hospital food was disgusting. I wasn't sure if it was supposed to be better or worse than airplane food. Not that I was familiar with how airplane food tasted.

There were about ten tables in the cafeteria, with four or five people at each one. I scanned and found an empty chair. As I headed over, I noticed there was only one other guy in the room; he was so muscular that his head—with veins bulging from his temples— looked too small for his body. Despite his massive size, he had a baby face, and looked like a lost little boy, staring down at his feet.

At the table with the empty chair was one woman—pale, about thirty, with long blonde hair and a face that was all cheekbones. Beside her was another woman, maybe in her mid-twenties, so emaciated that she sat in a wheelchair with a tube in her nose.

I'm not sick enough to be here. I'm not thin enough to be here.

"Fuck no way! Tony?" A familiar voice said. I turned around.

"April? Oh my God. I didn't realize that was you." She was beside the girl in the wheelchair. She looked like she had gained some weight.

"Do I look that different?" she asked. "Fuck, I know I got fatter."

"I didn't mean it like that."

"Whatever. You'll get fat too. Just wait." She snickered. "Sit down."

Seeing April was like getting a warm hug. I wasn't alone here.

"So when did you get here?" she said.

"Just this morning. How about you?"

"About a month ago."

"How did you end up here?"

"Oh God. I fainted on the sidewalk during a run. My parents said they said they didn't know what to do with me. How about you?"

"I passed out in my backyard. A friend found me."

"Very dramatic! I like it. Shit, you old people can still have fun, eh?" She laughed.

"That's so messed up."

"Listen, you're here too. So we're both messed up." She laughed again. I allowed myself a chuckle. Then she smacked my arm. "Oh my God, Tony—you bitch, you're so skinny! I'm so jelly!"

All the patients turned and looked at us.

"Oh shit," she giggled, covering her mouth. "I guess I shouldn't have said that so loud."

We sat down. I didn't know how to make small talk in this environment, but then from what I remembered, April was not the small-talk type.

"Do you know everyone here?" I asked her.

"Pretty much." The other ladies at the table looked at me while April made her introductions: "Kate, Andrea—this is Tony."

"Hi," Kate said. Andrea remained quiet.

"Most of the bulimics sit on this side of the cafe. The starvers sit on the other side," April explained.

"So is this like high school? There's some sort of hierarchy?"

"Nah. It's just like that. Probably because we all get divided by therapy group. All the anorexics end up in the same group. And then we end up together." She lowered her voice and leaned toward my ear. "Anyway, all anorexics are fucked up. At least we live a little."

"Damn, I miss that twisted sense of humour."

She smiled. "Thanks, I try."

A nurse came and dropped large plates of food at our table. "Roast chicken guys. Enjoy."

The meat was smothered in gravy and steamed in my face, pulling me in.

"What the hell," I said, "this portion is massive."

"Yeah. And you have to finish it. They don't let you *not* finish it." She started whispering again. "They check everything. Your napkins, under the plate, under the chair. Your pockets. And you know about the bathrooms right?"

"Fuck, so it *is* true."

April looked at me dead in the eyes, as serious as she's ever looked. "I need to get the fuck out of here."

I picked up my fork and knife and cut a piece of the chicken. With every bite my shoulders tightened and my palms got sweatier. I looked around and saw the other patients similarly looking anxiously at their food. Like this meal and every single one after it would be a battle. With each bite, fear rising; paranoia that each morsel would cause more of themselves to appear. Each of my swallows felt dry and laboured; I knew my throat had now become only a one-way street.

Chapter 36: Saturn

I woke up the next morning to find Dr. Khan, a young Indian doctor, humming some upbeat pop song while he scribbled onto a clipboard.

"Morning, big guy. It's eight a.m. Breakfast soon," he said.

"Morning."

"Do you know what day it is?"

"Wednesday, right?"

"Good. Do you know where you are?"

"St. Paul's?"

"How many of me do you see?"

"Umm ... one."

"Do you hear any other voices other than mine?"

"No."

"Okay, good."

He started humming to himself.

"Why are you asking me these questions?"

"It's just to make sure we're on the same planet."

He smiled at my look of confusion.

"Don't worry. If you were out in outer space somewhere—Saturn, Pluto or whatever—I'd find you and get you back. I wouldn't blame you. I think Saturn might be a kinder place than this world sometimes."

"Okay."

"How do you feel?"

"I'm okay."

"Tired at all?"

I felt energetic. It was strange but a nice change. "No, actually I don't feel too tired."

Dr. Khan nodded his head and grinned. "It's a nice feeling, eh? That's what eating does for you."

At breakfast, I realized it was easier to eat with people who shared the same struggles as me. In high school, when I was all stressed because the average to get into U of T was 88% or something, I'd purposely do all my homework in the library, never at home. Part of it was to get away from my mother nagging me ("You better get an A+—how are you going to get a good job without getting into university and how are you going to take care of me if you don't have a good job? You're going to take care of me, right? You won't leave me like everyone else? You'd never send me into an old age home like those white people, would you, Tony?"), but it was also just to be in the company of others doing homework—suffering—with you. We'd never talk to each other, but just a simple glance or two was enough to communicate, "I fucking hate homework too. I totally feel your pain." If someone smiled at me, it meant, "we're in this together, bruh."

That was what eating amongst fellow anorexics and bulimics felt like. A sense of shared struggle.

April was like sunshine. She added much needed light and humour to the place. She laughed and mocked the people having nervous breakdowns about not being able to finish their food. At first I'd condemn her for it, shaking my head and covering my face with my hand: "You know you're going to hell, right?"

"Guess what? You burn more calories in hell ... from the heat, you know?"

Soon, after sharing meal after meal with her, I learned to laugh with her, and started making the same jokes.

After breakfast, we went off into our therapy groups for the morning, which were a lot like the sessions at the Light House. There was one difference though: we weren't allowed to say certain words, for fear of "triggering" others. Words such as:

"Eating disorder"

"Bulimia"

"Anorexia"

"Starve/fast"

"Vomit/puke/purge"

It was also off-limits to say our weight out loud, or talk about calories or BMI.

So instead, we were learning about the body and nutrition, or working on CBT, using some of the same exercises I'd done at the Light House. There was this one interesting exercise called the "Exposure Hierarchy Ladder," where we had to record our levels of anxiety while working on an activity that might be challenging. The activity for the week was eating a heavy dessert, specifically a warmed brownie with ice cream, a departure from the Jell-O or arrowroot cookies we were used to having. We would have to record our level of anxiety on a scale of one to ten before taking the first bite. Kate couldn't hide her panic. Her lip quivering and her eyes near tears, she wrote a ten on her page, as most of us did. She took half a spoonful of brownie with a drop of ice cream and held it to her face. Then she shook her head and put the spoon down.

"Oh, God. I can't. This is really hard." A tear rolled down her cheek, her lip quivering.

"You can do this," Gladys said. "Just take a deep breath and go slow."

"You got this, Kate!" April cheered, shovelling the brownie into her mouth.

"How can you just eat it, no problem?" I asked April.

"We don't have a choice. We have to," she said.

In a quick swooping motion, Kate picked up the spoon again and put it into her mouth, closing her eyes.

"Great job!" Gladys said.

"Awesome," I said. Kate chewed the brownie slowly, and then smiled.

"Just one bite at a time," Gladys reassured her.

I too had written down a ten. I kept thinking about what April said.

She was right. I had no choice. I had to eat this. I had to eat it in order to understand that it wasn't going to kill me that I couldn't puke it out after.

Each bite was an exercise of rationalization. That this was just food, nothing more. That we needed each bite to sustain our strength. That we couldn't live without food. Sometimes, when I found myself struggling to finish, April would crack some dirty joke: "Tony, come on. Just put it in your mouth and swallow! We know you know how!" Gladys would giggle and then tell April to "hush your mouth, for goodness sake!"

I loved her jokes. I needed them.

By the end of the week, the anxiety levels I recorded had shrunk from ten to six. I could actually eat dessert without completely losing my shit.

Even as some of the CBT exercises started to work, I still cringed at the platitudes and clichés that came along with them. I loved joking with April about them.

"What are some the best clichés you've heard?" I asked her.

She smiled. "Hmmm. 'Just take it one day at a time.'"

"'Don't worry. It'll work itself out in the end,'" I said. "That's what people used to tell me when I talked about my mom dying. Yeah, totally worked out in the end."

"'It is what it is.'"

"I love that one. How about 'It's all in your head. Mind over matter.'"

"'Be present. Be aware.'"

"'The struggles you had in the past make you the person you are today.'"

"'Be kind to yourself.'"

"'Don't judge each moment, just *be* each moment.'"

We both burst out laughing at that last one.

"Ridiculous," I said.

April turned to me with a serious look. "So how do you like it here so far?"

"You know what, it's okay. I don't know how I would get by if you weren't here."

"If you wanna get out of here, you gotta change your attitude, Tony."

"How so?"

"You have to play the game. You have to pretend like you *want* to get better. And you have to eat."

"I know. But wait, aren't we supposed to actually want to get better?"

"Yeah. I guess. It's either that, or plan some great escape."

"That's so crazy."

"It is. But look at me—I've totally gained a ton of weight since I got here."

"And let me guess, you feel better about yourself? Like you never realized how beautiful you were all along?" I chuckled.

"Hell, no!" she said. "I feel like a fuck'n cow. Moo!" She moved in closer to my ear. "Mooo."

I laughed. "You know moo-moo is the Filipino word for monster?"

"It is?"

"Yup. Moo-moo."

"Well that's what I am—a big fat monster!" she said as she lifted her shirt, grabbing and jiggling some fat on her stomach.

We giggled like school kids.

"Don't you wish we had the drug thing? Or maybe an alcohol thing?" she asked.

"What?"

"You know, instead of an eating disorder, be a druggie or an alkie? It seems so much more glam."

"We'd be broke. Those problems are expensive."

"You're right. So practical you are. Plus, with all that alcohol we'd look totally bloated. I think I'll stick with yakking up my food, thank you very much."

Our jokes ceased when we saw a new patient—a teenage girl—being pushed in a wheelchair by her mother.

April fidgeted with the strings on her gown, and then looked at me. "You know, Tony, you might actually look good with some weight on you. You got a cute face. Nice eyes. I could just stare into them forever." She tilted her head and leaned into my face, and then burst into laughter again.

"Are you hitting on me? I'm gay you know."

"Well duh. There's a fucking disco ball over your head."

"Thanks."

She got up. "Don't flatter yourself. You're too short for me." She smiled and skipped down the hall to her room.

Chapter 37: GPS

"In our last session, you mentioned that when you start eating, you feel something come over you and you have to keep going?" Dr. Khan said.

"Yeah. It's like I get high or something," I replied. "And then I end up bingeing."

"Okay. So we need to find a way for you to get that feeling of satisfaction without overdoing it."

"I guess."

"Tony, I've treated many patients with similar cases. There's this diet—sorry it's not a diet—but a meal plan. It's totally vegan. Bill Clinton followed it, and he not only lost a bunch of weight, but he got a lot healthier, too."

"Vegan?"

"Yeah. I recommend it to some of my patients, some of whom have been these thin models, and it's worked for them. They eat as much as they want—well, they don't binge mind you—but a lot of vegan food is pretty healthy. So they didn't gain weight. You ever try it?"

"Vegan food? Not really."

"Try it out. There are all these hipster or millennial quote-unquote *cool* places to eat. The other day I went to that new vegan restaurant on Queen West ... I felt like I was eating chicken, but it was made of soybeans. The dish was called un-chicken and waffles. Can you believe that? Chicken made of soy. It was good. These millennials have figured it out," he said. "Anyway, I have the book about the meal plan in my other office. I'll bring it for you for next session. There's no harm in trying."

"Sure."

"Okay great," he said, scribbling more notes on his pad. "Do you have any hobbies, Tony?"

"I don't know."

"What do you mean?"

"I wouldn't know because I don't have time for them. I work two jobs."

"That reminds me, I talked with both your employers."

"You talked to them?"

"Yeah. Really nice people. Especially that Victor Melo—he seemed really concerned. I didn't share any information with them though, so don't worry."

"Okay, thanks."

"So back to hobbies. You have none?"

"I guess so. Unless it's eating," I said,

He smiled. "Let's try to get away from that as a hobby. What else do you *think* you would like?"

"Writing is my first love. Reading. Classical music. Movies too."

"Okay. Do you think you could commit to maybe writing every day or other day, or reading a book every few months, or watching or renting a movie or going to a symphony every week or every two weeks? Even at a slower frequency, no pressure. Do you think you'd enjoy that?"

"Probably."

"Great. Keep thinking about what you'd enjoy Tony. We'll try to figure out how you can add it into your schedule, even in small amounts."

"Okay. Are we done now?"

"Almost. Do you have a roommate? I don't remember if I knew that," he said, shuffling through my file.

"No."

"Do you have any friends? Or anybody special in particular?"

"No."

"Okay. You wanna talk about it?"

"No."

"Maybe next time."

"Maybe not."

"All right then." He chuckled.

"Are we done, Dr. Khan? Or do you have any pearls of wisdom or cliché lines that will be revelatory in my recovery?"

"No not really," Dr Khan smiled. "But before we finish, I want you to think about all that time you spend alone, and when it is that your head goes into those negative thoughts. Remember, boss, isolation can be a brainfuck sometimes. That's my pearl of wisdom."

"Isolation, eh? That must be why I changed the voice on my GPS to a male. Closest thing I have to a man," I said.

He laughed. It was nice to think Dr. Khan thought I was funny.

I always thought dreams were just thoughts stuck in the backs of our minds that for some reason couldn't make it into our consciousness. So sleep was a way for those lingering thoughts, matters or concerns to make themselves visible. As long as we could remember and decipher them when we woke up.

I might or might not have had a dream that night. Maybe two hours after curfew—which was strictly 9:30 p.m. every night—I heard the door knob turn, followed by a creaking sound. The hallway light caught the corner of my eye. Then a large mop of curly hair slowly blocked the light as it crept closer to me.

"April?"

"Tony?"

"What's happening? Everything okay?"

"I just came to say that I'm sorry, about what I said at the art class. I was being a real asshole."

"Umm ... that's okay. Don't worry about it."

"No, really. Sometimes I just say shit and I don't know what I'm talking about."

"It's fine. You better get back to your bed before they find you and we both get in shit."

April tiptoed toward the door and looked out into the hallway, and then came back.

She spoke with a sense of urgency. "Okay, good. Nobody there. I also wanted to say bye."

"Bye? Where are you going?"

"I'm getting discharged in the morning. My parents are coming to get me."

My heart sank. I cleared my throat. "That's good."

April handed me a piece of paper. "That's my cell and my email. Message me, okay?"

"Of course."

"Okay, gotta go." She leaned down and kissed me on the cheek. "Take care of yourself, Tony."

"Wait," I shouted as I leapt out of the bed. Suddenly April was gone, and someone else was standing in her place.

"Tony?"

"Yeah. Wait, who are you?"

"It's Gladys. I think you're dreaming a little loud there honey. Go back to sleep, okay?"

"Was I talking? Sorry. Yes, I'll go back to sleep now."

I laid my head back down and tried shutting my eyes.

Art class? What was April talking about?

Then I remembered. Earlier that day, we had gone over to the hospital's art therapy space. April had been looking forward to it all week. A couple of times a month, the eating disorder unit was given half a day to paint, read, write, sculpt or take a dance or yoga class. I thought how great it would have felt to rub this in my mother's face: if art was so useless, if gallivanting around "expressing myself," "doodling with paint" and "writing pretty poems," was too shameful a field for her son to pursue, then why was it being used in hospitals to rehabilitate people?

Our activity for the day was a simple watercolour painting. We had the option to get a canvas with a numbered outline and paint each section by number, or get a blank canvas and paint something in the room—such as bowl of fruit that was at the front table—or something completely from our imagination.

"I'm getting a blank one. Gonna make my own masterpiece. How about you, Tones?" April asked.

"Same I guess."

The art instructor was Zoe, a young white girl with big plastic glasses and stretcher earrings. "I'm going to play some calming music okay? If it's too loud, or if you don't like it, just let me know and I'll change it okay?" she said. "I'll just be kinda walking around to see how you're all doing, but what I want you to remember is that there are no judgments here, okay? Nobody is going to be a Picasso, so let's all be kind to one another and ourselves."

I liked her. She had this edge to her that made the clichés more palatable.

An hour later, April seemed pleased with herself. She came over holding the back side of her canvas toward me. "Hey Tony?"

"Yeah?"

"See the fruit at the front? How amazing does this look?"

She turned the canvas over to show her painting of the fruit in the bowl at the front of the room. "Isn't it so awesome? I'm so proud of it."

"Yeah, it's great." I said. But I didn't realize I'd said it without much enthusiasm.

It was actually nice to be in the hospital, because you didn't have to pretend to be well, or happy. You don't have press the "on" button for yourself and act a certain way. You didn't have to be a robot. You were *supposed* to be ill and depressed in the hospital.

So I could be myself.

"Jeez, thanks," April said rolling her eyes.

"What? Oh, I'm sorry, April. No, the painting is great. I'm just in shit mood."

Her tone suddenly turned hostile. "You're always in a shit mood."

"Well, sorry, that's just how I feel."

"Yeah, it's exhausting."

"I thought we could just be however we wanted around each other and that was okay."

"Whatever." She rolled her eyes again. "So what masterpiece did you come up with?"

She walked around my canvas. It was blank. What I'd initially thought might be fun had become a sad letdown. But it wasn't because of what Antonio had said to me; I wasn't paralyzed with fear that whatever I'd put on the canvas wouldn't turn out how I wanted. I couldn't put anything on the canvas because there was no picture in my head that I could reference. My head was empty.

"Nothing. You painted nothing," she said. "So who are you to judge?"

"I'm not judging."

April leaned in closer to me. "Do you ever think this whole act is a cry for attention?"

"What act?"

"The blank painting. The depression. The eating disorder. All a cry for attention, Tony. You have nobody in your life so you make yourself look sick to get someone to pay attention to you. Let's get real here."

"What are you talking about?" I stopped myself from raising my voice. I thought a joke might lighten the tension. "Did you take your bipolar meds today, April?" I laughed slightly, but she didn't laugh with me like I thought she would.

"You get all annoyed with platitudes and clichés and shit. You're just one big-ass cliché yourself. Gay, depressed and obsessed with your appearance. Fuck this." She turned around and rushed out of the classroom.

Zoe had come by just as April left. "Your canvas is blank, Tony."

"Yeah. I can't think of anything to paint."

"It happens," she'd replied. "You know, blank canvases scare the heck out of me too."

Later that night, the light flickering from the hallway caught my eye again. I heard the quick squeaking of a pair of rubber soles rushing up and down the hallway, then two pairs, then maybe three or four.

I heard things being said in a panic but could only piece together a few of the nurses' sentences:

"I can't lift her myself, can we get someone else in here?"

"Do you know if Dr. Khan is on call?"

"Oh my God, what did she do? There're staples all over the floor. Where's the box?"

Then sounds of more talking, more squeaking, the screeching wheels of a stretcher, doors being slammed, and finally a loud piercing scream. The kind that could break glass.

"Kate, get back to your room right now," a voice said. "Okay, Kate, calm down, let's take you back to your room." Then sobbing.

I got out of bed to see what was happening. I opened the door, and down the hallway was Kate crying into one of the nurses' arms. Farther down the hall, two more nurses were pushing a stretcher; the person—the body—on it was mostly covered with a white sheet, but a familiar mop of brown curly hair hung over the edge of the bed.

I started to panic too, only to fall and land on my right hip. "Fuck." Then the pain took over. Two feet appeared in front of me.

"Tony?" Gladys said.

"Yeah. Wait, who are you?"

"It's Gladys again. You fell out of bed. Go back to sleep, okay?"

She grabbed my hand and helped me get back into bed. My gown was soaked in sweat, which surprised me because I was always freezing in the hospital. She helped me change into a new one and tucked me back in. And all faded to black.

I sat alone at breakfast that morning. The day had a hazy cloud to it—the patients' faces were long, and even the nurses looked sad. April did not show up for breakfast.

Before heading into my first therapy group of the day, Dr. Khan passed me in the hallway.

"Hi, Tony," he said as he swiftly walked away.

"Dr. Khan? Dr. Khan?"

He stopped and turned. "Yes."

"Where's April?"

"I'm sorry, Tony. I can't give any information."

"She wasn't at breakfast. Did her parents come get her?"

Silence.

"Is she okay, at least?" I asked.

He walked toward me and whispered in my ear. "I'm sorry, I can't say anything." He started walking back in the same direction, only faster this time.

Then I realized.

"Did she hurt herself? Did she ... swallow something?" I asked.

He turned around, looked at me for a moment, and then kept walking down the hallway.

I wasn't feeling well during dinner that evening. The pasta they served was heavy. I looked down at my stomach; it stuck out over my pants. The pasta must have been six hundred calories. No wait, there were meatballs. Nine hundred for sure. Then some mango pudding for dessert. The ends of the meals were always the most difficult, especially since April was gone. There was nobody to cheer me on to clear my plate, or say, "just put it in your mouth and swallow!" That had always made me laugh. I looked at the empty chair across from me and tried to imagine the sound of her voice, but all I heard was the scraping of knives and forks from the nearby tables. I looked at Kate who sat beside me, having the same struggle. "It's just not the same without her. It's so sad," she said quietly.

The texture of the pudding was little less firm and more watery than Jell-O. I stared down at the plastic cup as I swirled my spoon around it; suddenly the remaining pudding looked like heavy globs of fat that were on their way to sticking to my body and face. My heart rate began to increase.

Why was I panicking? I had been doing well at mealtime the last couple of days. Dr. Khan said struggling between calm and panic when eating was normal though.

But I couldn't get myself to relax. I put the last spoonful of pudding in my mouth and looked around the cafeteria. Gladys was chatting down the south hall with another nurse. The bathrooms were down the other hall.

I checked to see that Gladys wasn't looking and scurried down the corridor. I tried to turn the knob of the bathroom door, but with no success.

Shit. I forgot. They would be locked for the next two hours. *Shit.* But there had to be other floors I could get to where they'd be open.

I turned around to check that the hallway behind me was empty. Gladys hadn't found me. I quickly walked to the elevator, looking as casual as possible. Nobody batted an eye when I got on and pushed the next floor down. I was still safe.

The sixth floor was the oncology unit.

Perfect. Their bathrooms always have to be open. Cancer patients are always nauseated.

I found a wheelchair-accessible washroom and locked the door. I felt like I was in some suspense movie, having managed a great escape.

I got on my knees and knelt in front of the toilet, just as I had done so many times before. The first purge was like releasing a caged bird that had been banging its head on the door. *Relief.*

The feeling didn't last. Before I could get the second batch out, I heard banging on the door, followed by Gladys's voice, furious.

"Tony, open this door right now!"

Fuck.

I couldn't look at Dr. Khan in the face later that evening.

"You do something like this again and you'll have to rethink whether you should be here."

I was looking at his stomach.

"Tony?"

I looked up at him. "Yes. I understand. I'm sorry, Dr. Khan. I don't know what came over me."

"Look, I know it's tough, especially when you feel alone now that April's not here. Remember how I said isolation can really mess with your head?"

"Yeah. Maybe I just need my GPS," I said, trying to lighten the mood with a joke.

"This isn't a joke. There are a lot of people on the waiting list to be here, who actually want to get better. Think about the opportunity you're wasting."

"Okay. Sorry."

Dr. Khan was right. April being gone made the halls seem darker. Time seemed slower over the next few days. My interest in things waned. I didn't want to go to art therapy, or play cards with anyone, or see what basic cable was showing on the blurry television.

Since I'd arrived at St. Paul's, I had successfully avoided staring at myself in the mirror. I was afraid of what I looked like having eaten full meals for five—or was it six—consecutive days. My face must have looked like a balloon.

One evening, I finally did take a look in the mirror in my room. I still looked emaciated. My skin was pale, my eyes sunken and yellow, my cheeks hollow, my collarbones protruding, my hair thinning ... I looked like myself, or some refraction of it.

Although my appearance hadn't changed, I felt myself looking *at* myself differently. Usually I held much pride and relief in looking as if I was wasting away—but this time I felt sorry, pitiful. Like the way I'd felt sorry for my mother when she was ill and suffering like an animal. All these things I felt looking back at my reflection—shame, anger, sadness—but most of all recognition.

I was looking in the mirror at my sick mother.

Maybe it was the lighting. The florescent lights of the hospital, which seemed to exaggerate every blemish and every vein, reminded me of the light in my mother's bedroom during the last few days she was alive. One afternoon, I had replaced the flickering florescent bulb on her ceiling. The new one seemed to highlight the jaundice in her eyes, which I rarely saw because at this point—eight months into her illness—she could barely keep them open. She couldn't sit up or walk, and her speech had deteriorated into grunts and murmurs. When her eyes were open, I'd ask her to follow my finger as I moved it left to right. She'd stare blankly, eyes still, lying on the bed. She could no longer see.

She'd stopped eating about a week before, so she was being fed through an IV, which the nurse taught me how to change regularly. She'd fuss with the IV once in a while, until she'd lose all energy and give up, and fall asleep. We didn't bother to confirm, but the doctor guessed that by that point she weighed at most sixty-eight pounds.

I'd say she didn't resemble a human being anymore. It was more like looking at something that sort of reminded me of a person I once knew and loved. Yet another refraction.

"The time is coming," her doctor told me, as the nurses looked on. "I'm sorry, Tony, but she doesn't look like she'll last much longer."

At the doctor's suggestion, I called the priest to give her final blessing. I called my aunt and cousins to visit as soon as they could. I called my mom's closest friends from her prayer group, asking them to pray for her; no longer to get well, but just for her not to feel any more pain. Over the next two days, many of them came to the house, with flowers and rosaries and religious statues, to see her one last time.

All her visitors told me that I had been caring for her wrong all along—everybody either had advice on what to do next or questioned everything I'd ever done.

"Why didn't you take her to the Philippines? The doctors there are so much better than in Canada. She'd be healed by now."

"You just need to recite this prayer every night, and she'll get better. Worked for my cousin's mother-in-law's cousin."

"Why didn't you try a spiritual healer? She probably would have been healed in a jiffy."

"You just need to give her this herbal tea and skim milk, and she'll get better. Worked for my sister's co-worker's uncle."

"You just need to read her this book and... "

"You just need to give her these vitamins and..."

"You just need to call my acupuncturist and..."

"Tony, you just need to ...”

"Tony, why didn't you ...?”

"Tony, you just need to ...”

"Tony, why didn't you ...?”

"Tony, you just need to ...”

"Tony, why didn't you ...?”

"Tony, you just need to ...”

My throat clenched with every magic solution vomited at me, all a bunch of jumbled words that meant nothing.

Apparently, everyone was a fucking doctor.

On the second day of visitors saying their last goodbyes, around 3:00 p.m., there was a half-hour window before another friend from mom's prayer group was due to arrive. I went into the bedroom room to see if she needed her dressing or her diaper changed, or if she wanted another blanket.

I sat on the bed beside her. Her breathing had become laborious and loud, which the doctor had attributed to her lungs slowing filling up. She sounded like a broken vacuum cleaner. A robot malfunctioning, its eyes fluttering open and shut.

Despite her unresponsiveness, I'd still talk to her. "Mommy, can you see my hand? Can you follow my finger with your eyes?" I moved it left to right. Nothing.

I decided to sit with her in silence for a few minutes. I looked out the window. The sun had melted the piles of snow completely. It was almost spring.

I felt something touch my arm.

My mom's hands were shaking and moving up my arms toward my hands.

"Mom. You moved your hands. That's great," I said, surprised and upbeat.

I grabbed both her hands and felt her squeeze a few times. She turned her head toward my face, eyelids slowly opening wide and staying open. Her breaths grew louder. It was the first sign of any responsiveness in weeks. I smiled in excitement and surprise.

"Mom, can you see me?"

Her pupils, buried in the yellow pool of jaundice, made contact with mine.

"Mom?"

The moment was short-lived. The pressure from her hands faded and her breath grew soft once more until it ceased. Her head dropped slowly to rest on the bed. Then her eyes, breaking their connection with mine, focused on nothing in particular, in the direction of the ceiling.

Her hands—that had once combed my hair and patted my shoulders and prepared feasts and clutched rosaries—were still resting in mine, but now limp.

It was only later that I realized she hadn't wanted to leave without saying goodbye. All morning and afternoon had gone by before I had come back into her room that day; she had waited for me.

Chapter 40: "All the Pretty Roses …" 2.0

84 Days Later

I'd never been one to claim I knew everything, or that anything was 100% certain—but I had one last secret that I believed was true (for me anyway): the more time passed, the more I knew that there was so much I didn't know. And all I knew was that I'd never know anything for sure.

I also knew that change was inevitable, whether it was positive or negative. Things change because they had to, in tandem with or in spite of my efforts. Change happened because nothing could stay the same forever.

Those were my few—albeit flimsy, intangible and, yes, cliché— pearls of wisdom.

I didn't know what would happen to me next. I didn't know if the last ninety days had "fixed" me. Or if it was even possible to be fixed. I didn't know if my newly learned eating patterns would lead me back to bingeing, or if a new diet would work, or if Lisa moving in with me would alleviate some of the isolation and financial burden. I didn't know how Victor would be when I went back to work, and what his reaction would be if I accidently called him "Jell-O," which I knew I shouldn't, because who the hell was I to judge.

And I had been judging him all this time.

I didn't know if Lauren had gotten a new job after being let go from Melo and Co. due to budget cuts, or if I'd get a response if I texted the number April had given me that night. I didn't know if the dentist would be able to save my cracked molar (which I had gotten used to eating with), or if it was too late to save, or if I could even financially afford to save it, and how much my bank accounts had gone into overdraft since I entered St. Paul's. I didn't know if the kids at Gold's would ask me where I had been, and what I would say.

I didn't know if the new twenty-five pounds I had gained during my treatment would stay on me, or multiply beyond my control and willingness to accept. I didn't know if all the journaling, replacement behaviours, mindfulness practice (or attempts, anyway)—all the pearls of wisdom, which I'd once thought were useless, from Leslie at the Light House, Dr. Tee, and Dr. Khan—had successfully been embedded into my brain. Or if I would still be cynical of all I'd learned, but continue try them anyway, hoping to prove myself wrong. Or if I would reject it all, like I had rejected food, and hope, and fond memories, as I had done before.

How was it that I had entered this place empty—of reason, sanity, wellbeing—only to leave full of questions and uncertainty?

What will I do when I get home? What will I do after that? Mind, come back. You've run away on me again. One day at a time.

The inpatient program at St. Paul's had ended. Nick came to the hospital to bring me home. The car ride was silent. Nick was never good at small talk. He kept fiddling with the radio until finally he turned it off and grabbed my hand.

"Tony, you know you can call me, right? For anything?" he said.

"I know. Thank you. And the same goes for you."

"Thanks, bruh."

"I haven't even asked you lately about Lucas."

"That's done."

"Oh, I'm sorry."

"It is what it is."

"What is it?"

"What is what?"

"The *it* in "*it* is what *it* is?" I said.

"Ha, dude I don't fucking know. It's just some shit people say."

I nodded.

We drove down Bloor, past the village, past Gold's Community Arts Centre.

I finally built up the courage to ask it. "So … how is Antonio? I never returned any of his texts or calls."

Nick kept his eyes on the road. "He left, Tony. He moved to Montreal. He got into that arts school."

"Oh."

"Yeah, he gave up the Miss Magic Mirror title, the prizes, everything. Then just shipped out and left. Chichi took over."

I turned away from Nick and stared at the road in front of us.

Be aware. Is that what I'm supposed to do at this moment? That's how mindfulness works, right? Don't judge the moment, but just be aware of it?

Nick looked at me and locked eyes. "I'm sorry he didn't wait for you, Tony."

We pulled up in front of my house. I followed Nick as he opened my door with my keys.

"Lisa has already moved most of her stuff into the second bedroom. She's doing a double shift tonight at the restaurant so you probably won't see her till morning," Nick said.

"Thanks."

"Do you want me to help you unpack? Maybe we can go get something to eat, if you're up for it?"

"No, I'm fine. I'd rather be alone. Thanks."

"Sorry I'm so awkward, bro. I never know what to say in situations."

"No worries."

"Lisa and I were like, 'should we put a sign up maybe? Welcome home from ED rehab?'" he smiled shyly. The thirteen-year-old boy in me remembered why I loved him. Before he left, he apologized for not having had time to clean up the backyard.

I was alone in the house. I opened the windows to let some fresh air in. I'd never seen the actual damage I had done to the backyard. I went outside.

The vines I had ripped from the ground lay in piles on top of the brown and yellow hay of grass. Red and brown petals lay scattered all over the lawn, some swirling in the wind. Winter was coming—I could feel the chill. I should have put on a jacket. Mom was always on me about that. I could still hear her voice, telling me she was worried that the flowers wouldn't bloom because of the crazy weather, and then later in the summer when she discovered the opened buds, saying she'd known they would bloom all along.

I could still hear her reciting one of her favourite phrases: "Flowers are God's way of showing us all the pretty things that life can be. You deserve all the pretty roses that life has to offer, Anthony. You deserve them all."

I could also hear Antonio saying the same phrase to me, in almost the same spot where she once stood, all those years later.

I collected the shovel, the axe, the shears and the empty bleach bottle and threw them into the garbage bin. I looked through the flower beds and decided I would go out the next day and pick up some soil to replace what had been poisoned. I gathered more shrubs and dead petals and leaves—many of the dried flowers crumbling through my fingers, flying out of my hands into the wind and back to the ground. They were so light and papery that I couldn't feel them. But I felt the sharp sensation of twigs and thorns scratching into my arms.

I went to the water hose to clean my hands off, the sunshine reflecting off the metal spout and catching my eye. The sun had found a hole through the cloud cover. Scanning the flower bed once again, I noticed there was a little vine growing upright in a corner. I dried my hands on my jeans and walked closer to it. A single rose was budding at the top. It was tiny, but the red was rich and vibrant as could be. I picked up all the dead foliage around it to clear its stage, washed my hands again, and went back into the house to unpack my things.

Acknowledgements

My heartfelt gratitude to the following individuals and organizations (in alphabetical order)—this book would not have been possible without you:

The late Aresio Adigue, Professor Kass Banning, CAMH (Toronto), Dr. Wayne Campbell, Sharon Chua, CIBC (in particular The HR PMO), Professor Michael Cobb, Edsel Colaco, Marlene da Costa, John DeBono, Aldwin Era aka "Chichi", Victoria Freeman, Neil Gagasan, Mary Auxi Guiao, Phil Hutchins, Justin Lau, Dr. Edward Lee, Mark Leslie Lefebvre, Erika Torres-Lyn & Sean Lyn, Lori MacIntyre, Sabrina Marino, Pamela Mauro, Rumi Meierhofer, Lee Moore, Bobby Nijjar, Alex Onave & Ricky Shi, Jeannette Padua, Melissa Paladines, Dr. David Robertson, Sergio Roque, Sheena's Place (Toronto), St. Michael's Hospital Mental Health Ward (Toronto), Nathan Tarrant, Adriana Tavares, Michael Tiqui and The Tiqui Family, The Toronto Western Hospital Mental Health and Addictions Department, The TLGTA, CGO Tennis & The GLTA, Mert Ulusoy, Anna Wilson and Frank Zappone.

To Martin Edralin, Ali Dean and Brittany Hadley, thank you for being the first editors of the earliest versions of this book. You are my diving bells and butterflies.

To Jess Shulman, thank you for helping me navigate the story and realize this dream.

To SoHee Yoo, thank you for your beautiful and unique vision.

To Isaac and Gabby, thank you for showing me all the beautiful things that life has to offer.

This book is dedicated to my mother, the late great Nelia Sotto and the ironwoman that is my sister, Arnelle Adigue.

Other Thank Yous and Permissions

Thank you to The Guildford Press for permission to reprint the exercise "Eating One Raisin: A First Taste of Mindfulness" from *The Mindful Way through Depression – Freeing yourself from Chronic Unhappiness* by Mark Williams, John Teasdale, Zindel Segal and Jon Kabat-Zinn, 2007.

Thank you to Victoria Freeman, MSW RSW, of Toronto, Canada, for permission to reprint the exercise "Body Checking/Body Avoidance". Freemantherapy.ca.

Thank you to The Centre for Clinical Interventions in Northbridge, Australia for permission to reprint and reference all other exercises. https://www.cci.health.wa.gov.au/Resources/Overview

Excerpt from "Mindfulness" from *The Mindful Way through Depression – Freeing yourself from Chronic Unhappiness* by Mark Williams, John Teasdale, Zindel Segal and Jon Kabat-Zinn, 2007, reprinted under terms of fair use.

About the Author

Jeffrey Sotto graduated from the University of Toronto, majoring in Cinema Studies and English. He was the screenwriter and script consultant of the Canadian short films The *Tragedy of Henry J. Bellini* (2010) and *Sara and Jim* (2010), respectively. *Cloud Cover* is his first book.

He lives in Toronto, Canada, and can be found on Facebook and Instagram at jeffrey_andre_s.

Printed in Great Britain
by Amazon